ONE. LAUNCH

Sometime soon...

"What a perfect day."

Jones looked across the calm South China Sea with the sun nearing its peak. All was quiet except for seagulls feeding near the sandbars or the occasional Chinese fishing boat.

Jones was pulling in a sensor, and in the distance, a bright flash lit the horizon. A few seconds passed, and he heard a dull 'BOOOM.' He looked and saw a small fire on the horizon, and the seagulls flew to his rear, as he looked back to see the turret on the Destroyer shift.

In his earphone: "All on alert. To stations."

He turned his patrol boat to return to the USS Trump, a US Navy Destroyer, half a mile away. Stealth technology had odd angles to hide the ship from submarines and look like a small boat to enemy radar. This new generation of destroyers combined the most advanced solutions of naval shipbuilding: railguns, lasers, stealth, modern power systems, and electronics. Over 400 feet in length, the Trump needed only a few dozen sailors on board, and everything else was automated.

Two sailors on deck ran inside.

A special ramp dropped to secure Jones' patrol boat. Jones ascended to the deck and was the lone sailor outside. In his earpiece, "Target map Delta India 3."

WHOOMP.

The radars popped up and scanned. Jones tripped backward. The turret's flaps rose and out, like a butterfly flexing its wings. The railgun shifted left and rose.

The turret shifted.

"Standby."

Jones's heart skipped a beat. He scanned the horizon, and the fire on the distant ship was blazing. More flashes and sounds in the distance and a dull "BOOOM, BOOOM" echoed.

The turret shifted.

Chief Petty Officer Adams spoke into his headset, "This is not a drill, Jones. Get down on your belly, take cover."

"Load spears."

The USS Trump had never fired the railgun in battle.

"Final check."

"Gun, OK."

THUMP

The first spear launched. The gun's heat and force were intense as it pushed Jones to the ground, scorched him, and blew out his eardrums. Jones lay still.

The spear is a meter-long bullet with a hard diamond tip that could pierce through the metal of any warship afloat. The spear screamed at Mach 7, punched through the Chinese ship's top deck, and through all decks with its blazing hot speed and super hard metal, creating a fireball and exploding everything in its path. The heat and force split the ship into two halves.

The satellites took control of the ship. Satellites calculated the points, angles, and times and sent data back to the USS Trump. With commands from Space, the ship turrets automatically changed the angles and loaded a new round. The ship became an entirely automated, massive floating robot.

WHIRZZ

The gun automatically changed the angle and raised its gun. The rounds loaded. The nuclear power plants on the ships synchronized, and massive energy fed the batteries and flywheels with more power for the railguns. These guns used electromagnetic force with enough electricity to light up New York to launch the round out at hypersonic speeds.

THUMP

Another round fired.

Four more strikes and the four navy ships locked down - the plan went into effect. The space satellites calculated new instructions to destroy thirty Chinese Navy ships. The ships were tracked; all thirty PLA ships were identified; the data lined up from the four ships, and the railguns adjusted for a new launch. The ship's energy systems, guns, and space communications locked into an automatic system. Now the 30 targets were locked.

Within one minute, the four ships fired 120 rounds. Within one minute, all thirty ships suffered strikes, 24 sunk, and six floating wrecks.

"End fire."

The command came over the intercom, but the computer might have as well-spoken it.

The American ships turned and scattered. They deployed six boats, each expanding a silhouette from light materials, with a range of electronic signals to deter a counterstrike.

"Open the deck."

Chief Petty Officer Adams found Jones mangled and fused into the deck.

"Oh, dear. I hope it was quick."

The Whitehouse – early morning

The guard on duty walked outside of the West Wing. In his earphone, "This is General Skykes. I am on the way over. Wake the President. Urgent."

"Yes, Sir," the guard walked to the President's bedroom and told the Secret Service Agent who went inside.

"Madam President, we have a naval action with China. It is serious."

President Cortez was still half asleep.

"Action in the South China Sea. We lost three destroyers and retaliated."

President Cortez slapped the pillow, "My God! Give me a minute." She put on her slippers and walked to the briefing room.

General Skykes arrived wearing jeans, a plaid shirt, and boots. "Madam President, Operation Sea Dragon was activated. We sank the entire fleet."

"Activated?" asked President Cortez.

"Yes, once it starts… it carries through to the end." The general smiled. "Total automation controlled by Space Force."

"The whole fleet?"

"The plan went into automatic execution."

"What does that mean?" Cortez was rubbing her eyes.

"Once activated, then within five minutes, we were able to wipe out all adversary ships in the region." Skykes smiled and strutted to the screen.

"Wait, they struck a few of our ships? What provoked this?" Cortez looked to the White House Chief of Staff who just entered.

"All rounds hit, and with the synchronization of the space sea and artificial intelligence, we pulled off a perfect assault!" Skykes laughed and pulled on his jeans, and walked to the podium. "Here is a view from our space, and as you can see, the targets are engaged, and within a one minute, all targets are destroyed."

Cortez stood and yelled, "My God, what have we done?"

"As you can see, the specific targets are engaged and as by design, and Madam President, the entire operation went perfectly as planned. Our investments in Defense spending are entirely perfect. We sank their entire fleet in the area. It was automatic." Skykes beamed.

"Yes, this shows the immense might of the US military." The Chief of Staff followed, "And the great investment in automation."

Cortez sat and grabbed her side, "Please stop. Get President Wang on the line."

"Madam President, that is not a good idea now."

"Who are you to say? I will do it myself. "and President Cortez left.

China – Zhong Nanhai.

President Wang sat frozen. "Who is leading the coup?"

Wang was tough and mighty. He was a special operations officer in the PLA who moved into politics when the political restructuring took place. His family was suspected of colluding with the Taiwanese. Still, now that the country was entirely unified, he used that previous weakness and built a financial and political empire. If there was ever to be a new Emperor in China, Wang was the one. Ruthless, cunning, and fearless - he moved up through the ranks - diabolical, daring. He never failed to finish off an opponent if the opportunity allowed.

Now, he was exposed.

Wang stood, pulled on his silk shirt. "Peng in the Politburo? General Wen turning the Army? Zhang? How could this happen on my watch?

The whole Navy wiped out, and now we have to put up with the foreign devils. Zhou, get in here now!"

Zhou met Wang as children in Hunan. Zhou was loyal beyond belief - proved when he threw himself into a gang to save Wang. He ended that brawl with over 100 stitches, broken bones, permanent injuries, and scars - his face would scare a psychopath.

"We need to find a way. Otherwise, Wen will kill you and take over before midnight," Zhou said.

"Wen is the most likely," Wang tugged at his collar.

Wen was the leader of China's military division covering Beijing and Inner Mongolia. It was one of the most critical positions, guarding against a Russian move but ideal for moving into Beijing.

"How can you be sure?" Zhou would follow any command from President Wang, his 'brother.' He would take the fall for the operation he was about to launch, and risk death for him and his family.

Wang's advisor rushed into the room. "This is Wen's actions. Admiral Wang confirmed that he provoked this fight in the South China Sea.

With one rogue ship and three rogue fighter jets, he attacked the USA and Philippine ships and caused this. He is making a move to get control of the strategic missiles."

"That evil..." Wang threw a crystal figure, a gift from the German Prime Minister, at the wall.

Zhou walked over to Wang, "He wants to bring the country down, take you out of power, and bring the country back to socialism."

Wang said, "I can't believe it." He walked and looked onto the courtyard in Zhongnanhai, the leader's compound at the Forbidden City in Beijing's Center. Wang saw soldiers lining up along the courtyard.

Zhou grabbed Wang and made him stand. "We must act now. Otherwise, the whole country will collapse into anarchy and ruin, the party will be ruined, and we will be blamed for the poverty of China. When the country is shamed like this, there is no end in possibilities. Our sons will likely be hanged or forced into humiliating servitude, and your daughter will be forced to live a life on the run. We must do whatever it takes."

Wang pulled the screen, rotated it, and said, "Freeze Strategic Assets, get here now, and get General Peng and Zhu," the Generals in charge of the missiles and Air Force.

Wang walked, "I can see Wen wanting to wipe out the Navy; it destroys his archenemy Admiral Zhang and throws things into chaos. What a raging, wild megalomaniac." Two soldiers came into the room for added protection.

"Zhou, go get this thing fixed. Cause a disturbance. Get the attention off the government, or we will be sweeping gutters in Pudong".

"Of course. We have control of the nuclear weapons for now, but the Land and Air Forces could shift to Wen. I think Zhu has already shifted" Zhou was always a step ahead of Wang and had a skill for cutting to the core issue quickly. "We need to do Operation CAT."

Wang had an iron face, never showing emotion under any circumstance – until now. Operation CAT was a brutal and vicious operation, and only a ruthless megalomaniac could call for it. Wang looked down.

"Yes, CAT." This was the sort of mission that Zhou could do better than anyone else-mass managed chaos.

Wang sat, "Kill and destroy …. for the greater good."

Zhou moved to inches from Wang and whispered, "Wen moves the 88th tank regiment into Beijing, and the air force is wavering. We have a few hours."

The head of the guards entered, "Three of the guards outside turned to Wen, and we killed them."

Zhou called the Fujian military district, Commissar Pang, second in command, related to Wang through his sister. "Launch operation CAT."

Pang stuttered, "Zhou, are you serious?" Pang knew that if he did not do as said or wavers in any way, his life and family's life is over.

"Launch it now. Immediately!" Zhou said. They heard gunfire in the courtyard.

General Huai ran into the room, "General Wen is moving the 88th Tank Regiment south. The Mayor of Beijing has turned against you, and the People's Hall and Tiananmen Square are cut off. CCTV has shut down all programming."

"Call my niece at CCTV, Get Wen to come to Zhong Nanhai. He will bring the Army here, and we will count his moves. Go!" Wang said.

"Wang, now, we do it and go."

Six soldiers entered, and they fled to the tunnel and stepped on a rail car to move to the bunkers beyond the Fragrant Hills, west of Beijing.

USA

John was cruising at 100 miles an hour in his BYD X88 driverless car.

"John, would you like to stop at Joe's today?" the 'car brain' said.

"Car, not today, big day." John was working on the screen on the side window.

"Joe is likely to make a trade with your wide receiver in his fantasy football." The brain was constantly checking John's fantasy league for opportunities and matching with John's actions.

John reached and sent a message across the car-to-car messaging system. He let go of the screen and leaned over to get a cup of coffee. "Oh no, no creamer." He touched a button to pre-order at the market. Depending on his route, it would be waiting or delivered by the time the Kardashian grandchildren special comes online.

John turned to check his display, "Yea, car take me to Joe's." He shifted in his seat, seatbelt groaning at the stress of 340 pounds and 20 years of adult pleasure.

Today was the end of five long years of preparation. John proved his new extravagant models for global warming tied to chaos theory and social behavior. His boss said this was ground-breaking work. The board was impressed, and funding approved on the spot - promotion, more staff, more money, and significantly more prestige. The sleepless nights and hardship, the obsessive, compulsive zeal paid off.

This promotion was also great news for John's wife Peggy - handbags, pearls, glitter, gaudy, loud, broad dresses. She might not like the hours and missing John for long periods, but John can take her whenever she wants to Europe and buy that home in the mountains. She can stay in Singapore while he works in the jungles of Sumatra.

"We interrupt the radio program for an important announcement."

"Forget that," John changed the channel looking for his football rankings.

Joe popped on the screen, "Hey man, you have a new phone."

"Yea, how do you know?"

"We got your car, and now it detects a new phone. Here is your order to go. The phone threw us off by three seconds. Maybe it will calibrate."

"Radio Z" the stations change, but it is the same announcer with more news of China in the seas near the Philippines."

"Car, change the radio," John says

"Sorry, John, this is mandatory," the car said.

The announcement said:

"We have initiated Operation Sea Dragon against the Chinese military. This morning, we neutralized the most lethal targets, threatening the world trade routes and our allies in the Philippines and Vietnam. In two hours, the coalition forces have sunk nearly the entire Chinese Navy surface fleet and the submarine force. We have offered terms of surrender and give them six hours to comply. China must now understand the price of peace and world order.

The local announcer said: "Well, folks, there you have it, we kicked some China butt."

"Wow, my tax dollars at work. Yea, hey, hey, hey." John was thrilled. "I want to get home and see this. Man, first the promotion, and now we are kicking ass around the world. Life is rocking, baby!"

Driving was an experience after that. Truckers were wavy arms out the window blowing horns car so loud it drowned out the radio program. He looked to the left and saw a beaming young guy in a family van, pumping his fist and yelling,

"Phone Peggy," the radio turns off, and the car calls home to his wife.

"Peggy, I have great news! What till you hear…"

"John, don't forget eggs, sugar, flour."

"Honey, I got my deal. Turn on the TV."

On the screen was a reminder to call Ping Zhen, John's partner in Shenzhen, China, who helped the past year with the project.

"Car, Zchat, Ping Zhen."

Upon the screen, Ping's face appeared, and three seconds later, contact. "Ping, so sorry to hear the news," John said,

"What news? The internet is slow today," Ping said.

"The navies in the ......" and the connection was lost.

"Car, get Ping."

"Trying, John. We are near Joe's now. Will forward to your ear pod when I get it", the car said.

The car turns into the lot, zips to a green spot, and self-parks in less than 10 seconds. The door pops up, and John pulls fat legs around and struggles.

"Car, assist."

Two prongs from the door reach down and grab John's shoulders and pull his body up. John does not think much of the help.

John entered the corner market, "Joe, did you hear about the attack?"

"Whoa," Joe is a 23-year-old bodybuilder. He jumped over the counter and ran to the window. He touched the glass and up popped an 80-inch program on the window.

"... the new rail gun technology was deployed to great success...."

"John, try out the new beer from Belgium," Joe gave one to John. "They say this beer can actually help you lose weight! some new ingredients."

"… Forty ships confirmed sunk….

Joe looked back and fascinated ….

John walked back, "OK, Joey, I swiped the credits at the counter, see you later!" He grabbed his items and out the door.

The USA – a high school

Amy was in the classroom and playing games on her phone. The teacher sat in the front, reading his phone.

The speakers in the room started, "This is principal Jackson. We will have a special assembly in 15 minutes."

Paul, next to Amy, said, "News, there is fighting in China!"

The teacher sat up, "Please everyone to the auditorium." He went back to reading his phone.

"Let me see."

"Yes, that is right. "

The other boys were excited. "Wow, great......"

--

The students gathered in the auditorium, and on the screen was the news. The satellite showed the spears' image splitting the ship in half, with a flash and the ship shattered and scattered, sinking to the bottom. The boys yelled.

The Physics teacher shouted, "Listen, this morning, a great victory, let's give it up for our Navy."

The boys start chanting "USA, USA."

"Hey, we gotta get this thing going. Sign me up!"

Amy tried to ignore the whole thing and whispered to her friend Sue, "This is garbage."

"One more time, give it up for the first responders."

Amy turned to Sue, "The problem is that these military are out there to destroy and kill in real life."

Sue said, "The military is here to grab our young men and women and put them in service, and when the time comes to tell our families that they are killed or maimed."

Bob said, "Oh, come on now, don't be dramatic. We have the best military in history."

"Whatever," Amy turned to her phone.

Sue said, "This is an excellent recruiting tool for the military. Last year ten boys signed up. "

President Cortez entered the screen. "The situations are ...."

The Principal turned the screen off, "OK class, we will end early today, Rise for the National Anthem. "

Bob said, "Thank god, we have our great military."

Another boy, "America is the greatest country on earth."

The assembled student sings the national anthem, and then boys shout, "USA, USA," and high five each other.

Sue said, "Now what?"

Amy said, "This is not a video game. Look at this ship, don't you think anyone is on it?"

Bob said, "Ha-ha, you do-gooder."

The Principal ended the assembly. As the students walk in the hallway, one Senior grabbed Amy, "don't cause trouble. You should be quiet and get along with your classmates."

Amy put her hands in her face and cried. She walked to a side room and called on her phone to John, "I am scared."

John said, "Meet me in five minutes. I am taking you home."

China

The military defeat was no more than a rumor. All news in China shifted to social issues and odd stories about domestic violence among movie stars. The cables beyond the shores were blocked, and satellite communication stopped except for the government and military.

Wang turned to Zhou and his guards, "America, you will feel our rage; you will suffer immensely. We will destroy you and grind up your children for fertilizer. Your family will be slaves and serve their new masters. Your entire race will be wiped out. We will kill you to the last man, woman, and child."

They all bowed.

Wang was very content. "Any nation not with us is against us."

Later that day, Wang spoke to his generals and staff:

"Any Chinese who does not do everything possible to pay back is a traitor and will be fed to pigs. Any leader that suggests negotiations will be shot dead on the spot, and his blood fed to his family."

TWO.
PERCEPTIONS

South China Sea

The USS Trump anchored near the Spratley Island, and Commander stepped on the boat to go to the island to accept the surrender.

As they approached, the Chinese Marines gathered and set up a flag of surrender to accept the boat. The translator approached, and the Captain saluted. Formalities were exchanged. The sailors and marines shared food and gifts. While the surrender was not the intention of the Chinese forces, the fact of the matter is that the situation gave no other option for either side.

Later that day, the Chinese gathered on one side with buildings, and there was set up a camp with support and water and food and some necessary barriers.

The US Sailors set up in the command center with only four sailors and one officer. New troops from the Philippines arrived that night, and there was no point in threats as the ship could stick a railgun bullet through a basketball hoop at any notice.

China

The Chinese Navy attacks were fresh but unknown except to a small group of leaders in China.

"Yes, will do!" Peng turned away from the screen.

"Damn if they won't do CAT," he thought to himself. Peng was one of only eight people who knew its scope, but he had the most challenging part. His whole career waited for this one moment. Peng sent the command by touch screen.

All commanders and staff were already on the highest alert. The commander keyed the instructions into the system. Thousands of smaller signals and instructions were spread to pilots, crew, other military bases, and warships.

In Fujian, pilots ran to the jets. In Terminal D, they slammed sledgehammers on the floor to expose an iron cover. Four strong soldiers took rods to turn the top. A small two-meter cubed hole in the ground lay a simple envelope and key for the vault – a museum piece, a piece of art. They went to the wall, smashed this open, twisted, and opened the vault. This extended into the hillside, a cavern full of crates and munitions. To the left were stacked three levels high sixty feet long, a long series of canisters with the words' rations on them. Only Pang knew the actual contents of these canisters.

"We launch operation CAT, humanitarian mission. Save China!" Pang said.

The rations are loaded on to eight of their aircraft, and on the cockpit are the targets.

One another mission, eight fighter aircraft turned to the Taiwan Straits and circled a US aircraft carrier.

The radars are lit up, and two Chinese fighters launched missiles. These two Chinese aircraft were quickly destroyed.

Below, four American fighters launched from the carrier.

The remaining six Chinese fighters fled back to the coast along Shantou, northern Guangdong.

The cockpits lit up with commands for the target area as they were chased by American aircraft fighters in China.

Further inland Chinese cargo planes with the rations from the bunker flew toward their own target area. The rations' delivery was automated with exact locations for the delivery. The pilot sat back as the plane flew on autopilot. Within 25 minutes, he approached the target and saw the beautiful countryside. "Things look normal here. Are you sure we have the right target?"

American fighters chased the six Chinese aircraft to the same target area.

Commands from the US screamed to the American pilots pursuing the Chinese planes: "Return at once! Do not pursue!" But it was too late.

The cargo planes dropped the canisters on a middle school, and the pilots looked back in horror as the packages explode, flames a hundred feet high.

"Uh-oh, what was that? What am I dropping?" The Chinese pilot tries to override the automatic system, but the rest of the payload is down.

"Oh… "The pilot screams and panics. "What the hell is that?"

Four more Chinese airplanes dropped similar canisters, and now the Chinese fighters and US fighters in pursuit fly over the exact same area.

All planes were overtaken by remote control. Three had malfunctions that turned the internal electronics against itself, causing explosions. The fourth made it further. The knockout mechanism did not work. It took a few more tries, and the electronics were overridden, and the plane dropped into a death spiral.

But the perspective from the ground was quite different…

Elsewhere in China

After the call to Fujian, Zhou placed calls to CCTV.

Urgent emergency priority – send a crew to specific coordinates and must be on station at 435 pm.

The Chief of Operations at CCTV called to the local station simultaneously - breaching protocol.

Urgent. Clear. Commands to get to a point on the ground, series of disturbances. Bring cameras and a reporter.

Xiao Wan, a local reporter, was an ordinary young reporter with just a few months' experience in the real world. She graduated from the Media University in Beijing with average grades and a lot of friends. She has big wide eyes, small lips, and perfect dimples. Xiao Wan was charismatic, well-loved by all who knew her.

She was not prepared for this story's magnitude and her life to come.

Camera crews from a local station scrambled to the same location. They set up cameras in time to see fighter aircraft flying, then the massive explosions across some farms. They are near enough to feel the heat from the fires.

Xiao Wen stops and says, "We go there. I will use the portables and…" She pulls out her kit of six flying drones that looked and flew like doves. Xiao Wen used these to fantastic effect when covering weddings and social events.

The 'doves' flew and sent broadcasts back to the local CCTV station. Xiao Wan had never seen violent death and now investigated a catastrophe, a disaster, smoke, fire, ...children!

"The horror!" Xiao Wen stood shocked in a panic, froze as she approached the school. Around her was chaos. The cameraman took over and guided the doves around the building, flying around trees, through windows. The images are getting more violent and dramatic.

"Xiao Wan," the cameraman shook her. He said again, "Xiao Wan, we have reports this was an American jet that dropped bombs."

Xiao Wan looked up, tears streaming down her face, makeup mixed with blush, and colors mixed on her cheeks. "We are here at Zhongshan middle school in Shantou, where the Americans have dropped bombs on...." she starts crying.

Xiao Wan wept as the drones sent gruesome images. Xiao Wan stood, cried, and choked up. She then screamed into the camera, "Children!!"

This report sent on CCTV instantly shook the nation. All television and internet channels switched to Xiao Wan's account.

This image of a 23-year-old beautiful reporter looking at the carnage became iconic. She threw her arms out, "Why?? Children!" and screamed. Nationwide in every home, this pain and suffering were transferred, and people began to wail. From Harbin to Hainan, Xinjiang, and Shenzhen, people beat the walls, screaming and calling for blood, revenge, and hatred. Images of children dead and burned controlled all channels, and all blame was placed on the American fighter jets that followed the Chinese jets.

The anchors on TV were very adept at making this into a firestorm of hatred. Sobbing mothers, screaming teens, and enraged fathers were interviewed on the major media networks for extended interviews. This quickly wiped out the bigger story of the defeat of the entire Chinese Navy - the humiliation and the subjugation of the military. This story turned to one of pure hatred and revenge - China would rise and crush the oppressors no matter what costs.

This tragedy brought forth years of humiliation and anger, the terrible descriptions from history, the thought that China needs to be in the rightful place as the Central Kingdom above all others – and bow to nobody.

There was an outpouring of over a million people in Beijing to flood Tiananmen square. The million people surround the tanks from the North, and the coup was stopped. The tanks from the 88th Regiment stopped, and the soldiers joined the citizens.

President Wang's plan CAT developed ten years previously worked. His goal of deflecting public opinion worked in his favor.

The camera crews built more detailed images of the school and sent it to CCTV. This news was broadcast non-stop every hour of every day. The horror-filled images shook every person to their bone. Their hatred and fierce determination to exact revenge drove everyone to scream the new mantra in China: "Save our children!!" This stew developed over time, and fermented into a fierce fire liquid, 200 proof hard liquor of hatred and resolve and determination to exact violent and final revenge.

They changed some of the graphics with CGI. By nighttime, the media was filled with horrific images of maiming, destruction, senseless killing. Small children with gruesome injuries. The CGI was not yet ready, but they showed the results. By the next morning, mobile phones were full of images of destruction and with the CGI filled into the show American planes, not their own. Where the original footage showed

Chinese MIG-78s, now they showed F-45 aircraft. The CGI was perfect.

China used these attacks from America in its state-run media. For the next month, there was constant coverage of the killing of children. People had to gather in town squares and swear their allegiance and hatred toward the foreign devils who made this attack.

"Not enough to win, has to be more than that," President Wang said to Zhou.

USA

In the USA, the media promoted grandness and supremacy, the military heroes, and the coming American supremacy and absolute security. People sang patriotic songs and could not get enough of the hero worship. Admirals were worshipped.

News and data out of China were blocked. Little notice was paid to the events in China and the people there screaming for revenge. That was all treated as a quaint reaction. The rage and hatred in China were of no concern as the sole superpower on earth had no fear, no desire for compromise. All reports and fierce hatred that escaped was noted as 'Fake News' and ignored.

A few minutes later, John pulled up to the school.

Amy hopped in the car, crying, "Please take me home."

"Yes," and John knew his daughter was sensitive to the news of the war. He caressed her shoulder and drove home.

As they pulled into the driveway, the garage door opened, and the car slid into its spot.

"Honey, did you hear the news?" John called to Peggy.

"John, baking two pies."

Amy ran to her room and shut the door.

"Oh, honey, I got the promotion."

Peggy said, "John, the Kardashian triplets were spray-painting the museum."

John was not listening. He was flicking the remote control but could not get it to work.

"John, the pies are in, and we can have some later. I am making some fettuccine for tonight."

"Damn these things," he pulled himself up for a minute, and finally walked over to the TV, and started by touching the screen. Up pops up a colorful menu, showing hundreds of channels but with some flicker. "Honey, we need a new screen."

"Jenny bought a 16k 130-inch screen last week. We need one. "

"Always trying to outspend Jenny, the neighbor two doors down." John thought and said nothing. "Ah, here we go," John said, and he touched the program on the left side, "this should be good."

… This morning, the Navy and Air Force of the coalition of the determined launched a counterattack. Initial reports say that half the Chinese Navy was sunk in less than one hour and were hit with complete surprise. The enemy navy had no chance against this well-planned and highly coordinated attack from Air, Sea, Land, and Space.

Now, we will go to the Pentagon for a briefing from the Chief of Staff, Admiral Hetch.

The Admiral walked to the podium. "The supremacy of the US military is absolute, and we are committed to peace worldwide." We will uphold the treaties and protect our allies from attack."

The press shuffled, and some shouted questions.

Admiral Hetch ignored them, "Our military is the best in the world. In one hour, we won the operation, and we are confident that there will be no retaliation. This will go down in history as the one-hour war. Perfectly coordinated missile and bomb strikes, lasers fired on key facilities, and command and control were taken out of action. Three carrier groups, six squadrons, submarines, and B2 bombers all hit at the same time. Over ninety percent of China's surface ships were wiped out. The submarine base in Sanya was turned into crumbling piles of mud and boulders. Complete almost instant victory. Nobody would dare take on the Navy, supreme master of the seas. From now on, there was one alternative, regionally, internationally."

The press shouted, and a colonel walked to the Admiral and whispered in his ear. They exited the press conference.

Colonel Philips took the podium, "Further details will be sent to you."

Later that day

"Here at Fox News, we now go to our military correspondent, retired four-star General John Smith..."

On Fox News, Maria, a hotshot reporter, age 28, the fast up and comer, was the most eligible woman profiled in Vogue - the media darling and with a considerable following. No doubt, she brought in billions of revenues for Fox and was being groomed for big things. 'Bigger than Oprah,' they said. She was dressed in a sharp outfit - one that showed her fabulous curves and athletic features. This complemented her guest, a retired two-star general, still fit 50'ish distinguished gentleman.

"General Smith, why now? It seemed that China was negotiating for a peaceful conclusion to this disagreement. Could you tell us what the operation did, how it was done, and what was the objective?"

"Sure, Maria. Here is a map of the South China Sea. We can see here on the East the

Philippines; West is Vietnam and South is here." The screen pulls up a 3D image of the area. "The Chinese Navy was situated here, here and here, with submarine bases here, here and here, and various airbases at Zhuhai, Hainan, etc......" As he pointed, the images popped forward with sound effects.

He turned to the screen and laughed, "At 3 AM, after we sank the fleet with railguns, 100 cruise missiles with guidance and equivalent of 2 thousand tons of explosives were delivered at crucial infrastructure. Our stealth planes and drones were launched a few hours before and targeted the various naval vessels here and here."

"General, did you say 2 thousand TONS of explosives."

"Yes, Maria, this is our new high impact non-nuclear explosives that we launch from high altitude. The impact is equivalent to a small nuclear weapon but without the radiation and stigma."

"Sir, I have never heard of this. Could you tell us about this new technology?"

"Well, this weapon has been on the drawing boards for some time and has been tested at length. It is one of the worst kept secrets, and this is the first time it has been used."

"Sir, we have a question on squitter." She pulled up a transparent screen. "How was this able to happen so fast, and why did we wait so long?"

"Ha-ha, well, I can't answer why we waited so long. You need to ask President Cortez that one." General Smith smiled, sat upright, and looked straight into the camera. "As far as the speed of success, well Maria is not so new, a concept developed based on 'Full Spectrum Dominance.' Our military gains control over all areas of land, air, sea, and space. We shut down their information sharing, the electromagnetic spectrum, and exploit this to our favor."

John watched the interview and wondered at the Kardashians painting the museum.

Peggy came, "John, dinner is ready." She frowned, "What is all that?"

In the studio, Maria asked, "General, it sounds like there is nothing they could have done."

General Smith turned to Maria, "Yes, Maria, these feed each other, and even if we can have partial dominance, we can achieve our objectives. With full dominance, we can completely shut down the other side, defeat any adversary, and control any situation across the full range of military and economical operations."

Maria asked, "Sir, doesn't this mean that in effect, we have built a global empire unequaled in history?"

Smith, shifted in his seat, "Maria, America is not an empire; we are a democracy…. But if we do have such an empire, it is because we believe in human rights and democracy. America is an exceptional country. We have a unique place in history, and our manifest destiny is to make the world a better place, to protect the causes of freedom, democracy, and justice worldwide."

Maria stayed on her questioning, "Sir, what do you think will be the reaction of the Chinese from a military standpoint? Can we expect retaliation? Are we safe here on American soil? Can they hit back and harm us now or in the future?"

The camera went to Smith, and he said, "Maria, there is really nothing they can do. They are castrated, and their military has been shown for the weakness that they have. They do not have the sophisticated weapons and command and control capabilities that the USA and its NATO allies have. This will set their military back one hundred years, and we will not need to worry about them in our lifetime."

General Smith smiled, and Maria sat stone-faced. "The Chinese will never be able to recover from this blow. Like the Japanese after World War Two, they will need to play by our rules and leave the South China Sea. Our allies in the area need to enter and administer the region."

Maria turned to the camera, "General, thank you very much."

Peggy grabbed the remote and turned off the news, "Rubbish."

John said, "Oh Peggy, look at what happened today near the Philippines. We won a big battle. It is thrilling."

"War, bombs, and killing. Stop looking at that." Peggy grabbed his arm. "Come, and let's eat."

John struggled from his seat and said, "Peggy, I have great news. My promotion is certain. My program got approved! We are moving up, darling!"

Peggy dropped the food, ran out, and jumped on John. John's full frame with Peggy weighing nearly 600 pounds. They slammed backward onto the couch, ripping the fabric in the back, and digging into the carpet. One leg of the chair was broken. Their poodle just missed getting crushed and ran to the bedroom. "John fantastic, wonderful. What does this mean?"

"Well, my work will come out into the open, it will benefit mankind, and we will be able to develop these new models we have been working so hard to perfect."

"John, silly boy, Money!! I mean, what does this mean? How much salary raise?"

"Ha-ha, well, probably 25 percent right away."

"That is all? After all, you are hard work? Jane's husband still makes more." Peggy frowned and pulled him to the dining room. "Amy! Dinner!"

John realized Peggy's greed, "There are other benefits, and we will get more time to travel, a new car and more benefits."

Peggy brought the casserole, "Well, OK, this is still good," She thought, 'With the new promotion that John received, they could look forward to more shopping trips, bags, teas…... They could move to a new school district, a bigger house, fancier car, and more travel. She could match Jane in perfumes, bags.

That night Peggy was in a better mood. She gave her husband a healthy look and grabbed him and gave him a good night. John went to work a happy man the next day.

The next morning, all the news overnight confirmed a complete victory - new reports of destruction in China, with bombings of buildings and bridges. John was in the car and in an excellent mood. Three hours of sleep did not deter his happiness. "Wow, we are still at it. Yea, baby, my tax dollars at work."

New York

Lord Saxon entered the room. Six foot six, 210 pounds of power. In his 50s, grey hair, distinguished, strong, Lord has the ultimate confidence – a genius inside a perfect body. As the head of the International Monetary Fund, members of royalty European, he made an entrance that people noticed - heads turned. There was a presence, a feeling of power, and a general fear as if some extra-human magic were about.

Here in the Federal Reserve Bank's basement in New York was over 3000 tons of gold bullion, stacked in plain view. This represented nearly all the gold bullion in the USA - gold piled five feet high, covering about 3000 square feet.

The boardroom was 150 feet long with exquisite art on Monet, Rembrandt, DaVinci, Michelangelo, and Warhol. The table was over 50 feet long, cut from a redwood tree – a one-piece, polished and gorgeous. Entering the room were the movers and shakers of the financial and corporate world. In walked the heads of JP Morgan and Bank of America Citi group, the London cartel, and European Central Bank.

The head of the New York Federal Reserve Bank stood to speak. "We will issue ten trillion more of fiat money backed by government laws and issued by your banks. You are to issue funds to support the new world order, new carbon mandates, socialist structures to crush the middle class, and gather up all their wealth into our hands."

The meeting continued…

"First order of business. Tom. We have a state that is pulling out their funds from the institutional accounts. - 1 trillion dollars – and looking to set up their own independent bank. They plan to fund their own infrastructure and set up a State Bank. The Governor is a real populist and an outsider."

"OK, we need to get those assets back under our system. Tom, you handle this one. The people love him."

Tom smiled and said, "What degree of harm?" Tom was the 'fixer,' 6 foot 4, 250 pure muscle, wearing a 500-dollar Italian suit.

Additional items on the agenda were set to rearrange the economy.

"GM needs a bump in sales, and China BYD needs a little takedown."

"How about we push 10 percent of BYD's sales over to GM?"

"Make it ten this year and twelve next."

The Lords of the world are determining the corporate and political landscape.

"You will need to coordinate with the banks and media to constrict credit flow and figure out news coverage. It should take just a few months to get this one done."

"Take Toyota down 20 percent, and we have some pump up for GM."

"Do we get our positions in the market timed properly?" By 'properly,' he meant time to play the options, call, puts, and fortunes to maximize wealth transfer the funds to their accounts.

"Lord Saxon, now the projects need to get control of some key technology for drone and aerospace guidance."

Saxon lit a cigar.

"We need to transfer some tech from Global Universal Enterprises to our friends in China."

"Find a useful idiot for his one - a greedy entrepreneur, driven mad by envy and jealousy."

"Joe will coordinate this."

Saxon exhaled smoke, "Keep this away from the Pentagon and State. After General Royse was ousted, we can't trust them to know this one."

"Yes, of course."

Saxon opened the phone. "OK, Senator, we need another stimulus plan to handle some economic enrichment projects. 20 trillion this time. This is a courtesy call. We have other ways to bypass the Treasury to come up with whatever money is needed. So, if you want some of that money, you know what to do."

"We will print this and issue 2 trillion for the team. Joe, take care of the distributions, and make sure you give enough for the politicians."

Senator Dixon said, "Lord Saxon, this stimulus and transfer of funds needs to go through a process. We must look at this. Last week, we had people digging into the details. "The Senator adjusted his tie. "Now, we need to take better care, and we need to increase the take on the other side."

Saxon leaned over, "Sure, Senator, you are right. You get this stimulus through, and the world is yours." And he turned off the phone.

The banker said, "Lord, you are a great man. How many things have you done for your country?"

They laughed.

"How did you get to be so wealthy and powerful and help so many people? You are a saint for sure."

Saxon sat back, "It's not about the level of money. It is how the national wealth is divided up. For the past almost three hundred years, we have had a failed experiment in America. We have let the masses decide the right thing to do. This has brought warfare, killings, poverty, and environmental destruction and commoners not understanding their place in society."

The bankers nodded and smiled.

"Now we will fix this situation and move into the New World Order, where all of society can progress; where the community can help each other; where the people are responsible for their neighbor; and they will share hardship and protect pleasure of the rightful elite."

Saxon stood and walked. "With no meddling by the little people. Let them fight among themselves for our small items and waste. Let them chant slogans about their miserable lives and debate about what matters."

The room laughed.

THREE. SYSTEMS

John goes to work

John woke, full of excitement.

His car audio system pulled down audio clips from the action in the Pacific. One of which was an interview with the US President.

"Madam President, could you tell us about the South China Sea."

"Thank you, Maria. After protracted negotiations and attempts to come to a peaceful settlement, President Wang of China launched an attack on our South China Sea forces."

"Madam President, have you spoken with President Wang?"

"We have reached out to President Wang and want to restore peace in the region. We will do what it takes for the interest of long-term peace. We will demilitarize and levy sanctions against China and ensure they never again rise as a threat in the world. Their Navy will be cut to two aircraft carriers confined to their coastal waters. They will be restricted to three air wings and will have no more nuclear weapons.

We demand that they shut down all nuclear power plants and enrichment, energy production is regulated and controlled. They will also need to pay reparations to the countries they attacked and turn over all silver and gold bullion to the International Monetary Fund."

"Do you think this is harsh, that China will retaliate?"

"No, Maria, China cannot retaliate. We have reduced the threat and are on the highest alert against any further danger. China must comply."

"Thank you, Madam President. This is Maria of …."

When John arrived at the office, he looked at his little cubicle and thought how much he will enjoy a new office. He walked around the floor and saw his research partner Stanley Thomas.

"Look at you, I see you got the promotion, congratulations," Stanley said

"Thank you, Stanley. I know I couldn't have done it without you."

"Yes, John, you are right, I did most of the work, and you got the credit."

"Now, come on, Stanley, you gathered a lot of data, but it was the calculations...."

"John. Chill enjoy your new position, and don't forget the people who helped you rise," Stanley walked past him and gave a shoulder bump on the way.

John looked over the new office space and started to plan out his staff acquisitions.

Inner Space

The G11 jet flew from New York to Beijing in less than 90 minutes at speeds of Mach6 and in sub orbit at Mach 20. Space travel was ready to go mainstream, but production was scaled back with the new carbon trading plans. Now, only official travel was allowed.

Lord Saxon leaned back in his chair, sipping a 24-year-old scotch. Today the pilot was Captain Thom, a former Air Force pilot who flew B6 strikes over Turkmenistan.

Lord Saxon reviewed documents to establish a new order for the Chinese and guarantee the world order. Traveling with Lord Saxon were Alexander Jones, the head of the New York Federal Reserve Bank, and General Fultz, the Deputy Commanding Officer of NATO.

The G11 descended and made a relatively easy landing, entirely guided by the automatic controls. The Beijing Nan Yuan airport, a converted Air Force base, was something out of the 1960's - basic, no amenities, grimy tiles.

Saxon said, "Well, let us go get them."

They exited the aircraft and, on the tarmac, met a 30ish young beautiful Chinese woman, exquisite silk clothes, with an athletic frame. She had no smile at all, piercing eyes, striking beauty, muscular calf muscles, and flawless skin. "Lord, Gentlemen, welcome to Beijing. Please come this way. We are pleased to see you, and anything we can do to make your stay better, I will be your guide."

Lord was thinking other thoughts for sure. She held his hand and guided them to two limousines in the yard. The cars moved into a hangar, and two identical cars were exited to act as decoys. Saxon's cars entered a tunnel, and they moved quickly under Beijing. The decoy cars went to the Diao Yutai Guesthouse.

Virginia, Defense Intelligence Agency

"Sir, we are tracking a G11 and have lost the passengers but can only confirm one of them looks to be Jones from the New York Fed. We do not know the others."

Beijing China

Saxon's cars emerge near Tiananmen Square, past the Great Hall of the people, another few turns and into Zhong Nanhai. The vehicle entered a building, and the China Central Bank Head, Zhang Yuxin, and People's Liberation Army Commander, Zhou Xin approach.

Saxon said, "We came here to show our respect and to make it clear with you that we are very serious about this cooperation."

Zhang said, "Lord Saxon, you are very welcome in China. We aim to have fruitful cooperation."

"Likewise," said Saxon while Jones and Fultz shook hands with Zhang and Zhou.

"Come and let's sit and have some tea," Zhang said as they walked. "Lord Saxon, we are anxious about what this American government is doing to us. We think it will destroy the world order we worked so hard to implement and cooperate."

Lord Saxon said, "General Zhou, you know General Fultz, the Deputy NATO Commander and Commander of the Belgian Armed forces. He will work with you to ensure peace and stability and commit to you that we are partners in the New World Order. We cannot do it without you."

General Zhou said, "You know, one of our Navy Captains made a mistake and sank your ships in the South China Sea. Your response was far too strong."

General Fultz said, "Our response was automatic and should not have been so strong. It's the new warfare driven by data."

Zhou said, "The Hague Court and NATO gave us the green light to take care of our own region. Then your American Navy wiped out our fleet in the South China Sea."

Saxon said, "We will put some barriers so that the response is not automatic."

Zhou was skeptical, and he looked at Saxon, "Yes, let us hope."

President Wang walked into the room. Everyone stood, and President Wang walked and said, "Now you impose all these technology restrictions on us. We cannot have any nuclear power. Our Navy cannot be rebuilt, restrictions on our aircraft, size of the Army, technology, etc. How are we to be a partner in this order if we cannot defend ourselves?"

Fultz said, "This was a radical reaction from the United States, not NATO."

Saxon said, "We will work it out. Let's not escalate."

Wang turned to the New York Federal Reserve leader, "Mr. Jones, how are we to operate in this world that is dominated by New York and London? The English-speaking world will rule for the next 1000 years, and our children will be slaves to their whims. We must have cooperation."

Jones said, "Please call me Alex. We have companies that will help you to advance beyond the restrictions. In fact, we are here to build you up, not tear you down."

President Wang said, "We need more trade and not less." He paused, "Especially open to sharing technology. You know China invented many things that have changed the world."

Jones said, "We have big ambitions and are working hard to bring the Central Bank in with the international system."

Lord Saxon said, "Do not worry about those government restrictions. When the new session is in place, you will see. We know you are a vital partner…. And we see your role as especially important..."

Jones said, "The Federal Reserve supports you. The politicians have been trying to keep control of the money supply in their hands."

President Wang said, "Gentlemen, thank you for your visit. We will resolve these issues, but to reach a new peace, we expect to see some concessions now."

Lord Saxon said, "In the end, we will build conflict and confusion in our own populations while we work behind the scenes for the New World Order that is needed for real progress."

Wang said, "Yes, that is the spirit. We will play the role for the public. Get that whiskey over here and let's toast".

The group said pleasantries, and President Wang left the meeting.

Later that day

Late morning, John's boss arrived. "John, come here and let us sort out the arrangements. In addition to your program, you are assigned to work on a unique project. We have been tasked to manage a drill for the department of population security. You will be helping with this and using the tools you invented. This is all hands-on deck. We need you to manage this drill, and you are the only one here with a Top-Secret clearance and expertise.

"Oh, boss, sure will do." This was out of John's area of expertise and made him worry. "How are we going to use the tools for this? I built that up for CO_2, not for this. The social engineering aspect,

"You still have the pay raise, but we must set up the program and get started. John, we will set you up in your office and staff now. Here is the plan. We are participating in this drill to see the reaction of the population to a solar flare - to see what they will do in reaction to media reports. We need you to organize the work and get it out to the media."

"In any case, I will adapt." John grabbed his tie.

His boss pulled him to a side room, "Ok, here is the program. Look at these graphics."

The walls and ceilings were covered with interactive paper that doubled as a television screen in the room. A few years ago, an engineer from India developed a new fabric that mimicked high definition TV. The entire wall ran TV programs, computer programs, etc.... In the past year, some engineers developed software that would reach out to figure out the dimensions so that the new wall TV could be any size.

"Let us start the solar flare video simulations." On the wall was the sun at eight feet high, and then came a series of flares, bubbling up, huge bursts, and more flares.

"John, look at these graphics. Aren't they gorgeous? Here are the graphics from the earth, and then we make some from the Groves telescope. Pretty authentic, isn't it?"

John said, "I never saw such realism."

"These designers are straight from the best of the best of Hollywood. Four studios handle different overlays, and our team here puts them all together. They think this is for an upcoming movie that we are funding on the sly," He had a twinkle in his eye, proud of himself.

John walked to the wall, "Never imagined the Hollywood guys could make this."

"See, there is the flare itself. We ran a series of reactions and simulated the results, getting some large flares. Now over here." And on the second wall were the planets, from the perspective of the sun. Then the program focused on the Earth. John stood at the left, and the sun on the main wall, the flare explodes and shoots toward the Earth.

Stanley turned on the filter to show the magnetic field of the Earth. The flare engulfs the area, shaking it, pushing, pulling the field.

"Ok, zero in on the earth," the boss walked next to John and put a hand on his shoulder. "Wait, we have to pull that simulation up from another program. Before that, here we have a series of twelve flares, various closeness to the earth, and then this flare hits it straight on. There are massive flare power strikes hitting the whole northern hemisphere—Russia, Canada, two on the USA, Japan, Northern Europe, and the UK."

John said, "Suppose the flare comes out, and at what point will this wipe out the electronics and telecommunications."

Stanley said, "John, we will be simulating levels of destruction. The electric grid will be fried, with nearly every power station, substation, either shut down or exploding."

Beijing

"President Wang, the ten thousand eyes project, is making progress.

"Yes, but that is just whales."

"Sir, Initially, this was made as a program to track whales, but these things can track all large objects' movements. We have achieved excellent dual-use."

"Tell more," Wang sat back.

"They relay the information to each other in a network. Each will send back to the other until it hits a super eye, processing all the information. Each problem looks like a small fish of about two feet in length and can sense all movements in the ocean. The prime object is nuclear submarines, especially the missile launchers. So, these probes are launched from Shandong, and they can stay underwater for over ten years. They are hard to detect, and even if detected, they are nearly impossible to neutralize. Even if thousands of these are taken out, then there will always be more. So, these probes are floating around, emphasizing the likely locations that a submarine would be located. They will float there, moving slowly and methodically, like any other fish. One in a while, a shark may mistake one for a fish, but the shark would find it quite unappetizing, or worse, deadly to swallow one of these."

"Sounds complicated."

"Yes, agree. Our scientists have achieved the impossible." He gave the report to the President. "The probes can track moving objects and send a low power signal to the others. The thing that makes this fish work is the relay of information, as they not only see and send what they have, but they can collect and forward from other fish. Then there is a mechanism for the computer to cancel out redundancies. By the time, a supernode gets the information, they have a reasonably good idea.

The supernodes are in the hundreds and relay the crucial information onto the data centers back in the motherland.

The powerful robots are squid-like drones that swim like a squid and hover around some areas out of whales. As mentioned before about the fish, the whales could swallow and suffer a terrible death, more so than sharks. Inside the squids are quite useful explosives. Too high heat, like thermite, can burn through anything with no known remedy from such attention.

As the trials were being launched, the squids were launched. The fish's data was elevated, the signals relatively higher, and under cover of a whale census exercise. Much more low-frequency signals in the water, sure to stir some attention from the targets, so they were under this cover.

The data collected was quite useful and accurate, fed to the keen eyes, fed back to land, and processed. Once the target was approved, the sharp eyes became the guidance nodes and automatically guided the squids onto the targets, being the submarines.

New York

Maria did not have any problem getting a man. She could have any sports star, movie star, or business tycoon and was regularly on the gossip pages of the NY Post. Maria was unique in the world, recognizable in every country to the remote parts of Borneo.

Maria's brand was her work life, high flying, risk-taking, her iron will, and discipline. Maria had charm but could be tough as nails. She fearlessly tracked down criminals, white-collar that is, and exposed corruption in business and government. Maria loved to produce hard-hitting investigations on the inner workings of companies. She exposed securities fraud and collusion among three of the five biggest banks. Her reporting won her a Pulitzer and led to the conviction of four executives.

This interview about to start had Maria a little on edge. Lord Saxon has not been interviewed for five months.

Maria skipped saying hello. "Lord Saxon, can you tell me about financial programs where the Federal Reserve creates money out of thin air? It indeed uses national public credit to lend to your companies and banks at interest, then buys real assets?"

Lord Saxon was furious but kept his appearance steady, "Ms. Maria, There is always an under currency of conspiracy theories. All money comes from the government. We do not print money."

Maria leaned forward, "But Lord, in fact, the treasury prints the actual notes, but you then lend those into select banks at interest. You are taking the national credit and stealing it."

Lord Saxon said, "Stealing? You are mad. This is silly. How can we do that? Money comes from the economy; it comes from people's skills and expertise."

"But stealing is what it is." Maria kept pushing for an answer, thinking, "This will land a

Pulitzer, no doubt; I got this guy now. Making my way on up the ladder."

Saxon laughed, "Oh, Maria, that is simply a fairy tale. I am afraid you are speaking rubbish."

Maria could sense unease, "Fine. On another matter, we heard from a reliable source that you recently visited Beijing to have talks with the President of China. Could you tell us what those talks were about?"

Lord Saxon, in all situations, showed a remarkable ability to control his facial muscles. Still, this time he turned to his left, and his face turned red. "Well, that is ridiculous. Where have you heard of such nonsense?"

At that moment, the feed ended, and there was a commercial break.

Lord Saxon stood, "I will not be insulted with false allegations… You call this journalism?"

Maria stood, "I have good rock-solid sources."

Saxon walked back to her. "Maria, you are living a pack of lies."

Maria said, "Lord Saxon, we still have another segment."

Saxon said, "We came here to talk about the charity work with the Kentucky home for children. You hatched an ambush." He pushed a button on his phone. He said, "football." Immediately two large bodyguards arrived.

Maria said, "You cannot do this; this is a live show."

More guards rushed in and presented credentials to the producer. The set started to shut down. One guard went to the camera and placed a hood over it. Another pulled the electricity, and a third stood guard with his pistol drawn.

Upstairs, the producer called "backup," and they switched over to a replay of an old segment.

Saxon said, "Damn, why did I agree to go live?" He motioned to four more bodyguards to block the doors. The first two returned.

The show producer ran forward, "Maria, you need to come in and have a little talk."

Maria felt tightness in her gut, thinking, "Oh, I have never seen things move so quickly."

Saxon walked away, yelling, "Get the CEO. Get him in here now!"

"Sir, he is in an analyst meeting."

"Now!"

In two minutes, the CEO arrived on the floor, "What is the problem?"

Saxon walked to him. "You ambush me. We had a segment on the charity, and she hits me with fantasies that are nothing of interest to her or the public. This is an outrage and shows you do not run a tight ship. I want justice handed out, and this dealt with."

"Come now, Lord, Maria is a good team member. Let me talk with her. She will never do this again".

Lord left the set and turned to one of the bodyguards, "Tom, clean up this mess."

Tom stepped forward. "Yes, how high?"

"Her out of the industry, shut up and dealt with at the right time. She is now discredited, and we need every media person to understand specific areas will not be questioned."

He called the CEO, "You handle this."

"Come on, she was just a journalist."

"Ok, you know what, CEO. Let us handle this, and we won't bother you with this." He looks at him; the eyes get small, voice hissing. "You run your company as you wish."

They left through the side elevator.

In the basement, Lord Saxon was in his car and called Tom. "Put this out into action. I want to see results in a day."

Nellis Air Force Base, Nevada

"General Madden, the stealth planes look like spaceships." President Cortez was making a visit to the West.

"Madam President, their design made the aircraft invisible to all known radars and aircraft. Now we have the decisive advantage. With these, we can swarm all enemy aircraft, and we have total air superiority."

President Cortez said, "The new fighters cost one billion dollars per plane."

The General sputtered, "Madam President, the new stealth technology makes the aircraft small on enemy radar, absorbs radar, gives off no heat signature, reduces the sound to zero, and gives a silhouette that confuses all enemy systems. With new sensors, it can easily detect all enemy systems."

"Still, why do we need to borrow money to build these aircraft?"

The General stuttered, "Borrow? We don't borrow." He looked around. "The new aircraft is designed to protect pilots from the sudden loss of consciousness. The cockpit was also overhauled to improve pilot safety. A new backup oxygen supply system was also included to give better life support and allow pilots to fly under higher G forces."

President Cortez asked, "Yes, but why do we need to borrow money to pay for these?"

General Madden was silent and looked at the President. "Each cost only one billion dollars, and each hour in the air is less than one hundred thousand dollars. The pilots are trained, and no enemy aircraft has ever breached within 200 miles."

The President turned to him and said, "I do not doubt the quality of the aircraft. Why do we need to borrow the money from a private bank, the Federal Reserve?"

The General said, "Madam President, the Federal Reserve Bank is a government bank. That is why it says Federal. The F55 is ready for the future war against any adversary. This is going to be a revolutionary new step for combat fighter tactics with the latest technology. We are at least 20 years ahead of our closest rival."

Later that day

President Cortez was in the middle of a press conference and discussed the money system. "The United States can issue its own debt-free United States Treasury backed money. We will no longer borrow from private banks and then pay interest. If you look at the amounts we have borrowed and the amount of interest we have already repaid, you see it is more than the tens of trillions of America's wealth. We have an enormous debt that can never be repaid under the Federal Reserve system of money. That came from debt backed money and will remain so. But from now on, we will also issue United States Government notes backed by USA government assets. You can be confident that your money is safe as can be with government money."

New York

Lord Saxon sat at his desk with Alexander Jones and the leaders of three large banks.

His Chief of Staff kicked open the door, "STOP!!

Lord Saxon jumped back, and the other two ran to the opposite walls covering their face.

He ran to the screen and turned it on, "Look at this!! Look at this announcement from Cortez. She will move to US Government Treasury issued money!!"

Saxon said, "Never!!" He threw his phone against the wall. "Only Federal Reserve Notes will do."

"Sir, are you fine?" The Saxon's secretary ran in. "Your blood pressure is hitting dangerous levels," Saxon's nurse rushed to him and tried to grab his arm.

"How dare Cortez do this. Who the hell does she think she is? We put her in to control that White House office. We own her. That trash!! We will kill her!!"

"Please, Sir, have a seat."

To his secretary, Saxon said, "Call President Wang now." He stormed out.

Hong Kong

The Ambassador from China entered the hotel suite.

The African Minister said, "We do not have any benefit from your investment. You used all these funds, and you took them right back and hired your own contractors at inflated rates. This is corruption and graft. Far over budget, and there was no way to stop your contractors."

The China Ambassador said, "Minister, this is the agreement when we made the deal. You agreed that you had to have a certain level of quality. We made a deal, and it is part of the contract."

The Minister walked forward, "Come now, we are friends, you remember all the good times we enjoyed together in Thailand. You are raping my country, you pushed this easy credit money on us when we were starving, and now you look to steal all our natural resources. You are raping our country now. You are sucking all the iron ore out of our land, and now we cannot even use that trade to earn foreign dollars to pay the bills. This is s a game you are playing."

The Ambassador said, "Minister, all we ask is that you pay us in kind. You do not need to repay with dollars. We can work something out with resources, and you will be rewarded in an offshore account and placement of your child at Harvard."

The Minister sat down, "Ok, let us go to the Africa conference in one month, and we will work this out."

John's home.

"Daddy, did you know that the United States never landed on the moon?" Amy walked to the kitchen to get a pop tart.

"Oh, Honey, that's great." John found a folder in his briefcase.

Amy walked back, "Yes, it was all fake. It's in the textbook."

John said, "Textbook? If it's in the textbook, then it must be true." John opened the folder.

Amy walked to her room, "Thanks Daddy, China was the first country to land on the moon."

John continued to ignore his daughter, "Hmm, this script has an odd name on it, not mine. Must have been mixed up." John opened the folder. He read the file and saw plans that looked like a movie script and a project plan with dates and assignments. He read about a series of deep solar flares of incredible magnitude released into the direction of the Earth. Starting at H hour, the media will make announcements. There will be a series of news announcements, morning talk shows, even jokes written for late-night comedy. Various experts will come on, with some alternative announcers who will announce gloom and doom.

John mumbled to himself, "Impressive, there is a 'Department of Population Security' to collect all those people's names and reactions of social media."

John could hear Amy watching television, and he shut the door. "Ok, here we go," John remembered the simulation.

He read more instructions: Then, the solar flare will hit the earth, and we will measure the people's reaction. Here there is a drill to take down North Carolina and Nebraska that are supposedly hit by the flare. John mumbled, "Oh, that is interesting, and we will gather the date from the Emergency Management people there."

John shook as he read the simulation that covered the destruction of the United States of America and the enslavement of the population.

Under the Pacific Ocean

The bio tags for whale tracking became an excellent selling solution for all kinds of tags. It was lauded as another technology breakthrough, that this incredible device that helped track whales, any animal, or any living being.

The artificial squids 'swam' from Qingdao. Thousands of probes dropped from thousands of fishing boats worldwide, and the sensors were free to float among the various drifts. They randomly floated around the ocean, sending sonar signals looking for large objects.

As the whales were tracked, the device sent networked low-frequency sonar. Data was collected in distributed databases worldwide among the other sensors. If a sensor was captured, its data was encrypted and impossible to open in any reasonable time. The data worked alone and part of a network adding to a massive dataset with location, time, and conditions. The probes stayed underwater, feeding off saltwater as an energy source and no need for other energy to sustain itself.

After a few weeks, two probes working near each other found another target: USS Halsey, a nuclear missile submarine 800 meters submerged east of the Philippines.

FOUR. TRANSFER

South China Sea

The Chinese Navy ship passed and stopped between the USS Trump and the island. The US sailors and Marines prepared to transfer the Chinese sailors and Marines from the island.

Two Chinese fishing boats approached and stopped a mile away from the Navy ships. All ships sat quietly for one hour. Then sailors poured gasoline on the deck. A man fired a flare, and half the deck went up in flames. A speed boat came forward and collected the sailors. As they raced off, the ship slowly sank.

An aircraft approached from the north and flew over the sailors. The plane had Chinese markings, and the sailors cheered.

The aircraft returned and fired cannon at the Chinese prisoners and killed thirty-three, Chinese sailors.

The men on the USS Trump watched and called up to get permission to destroy the aircraft.

Underwater, the sunken Chinese ship side opened, and three large snake-like devises exited and sat on the floor of the lagoon. These started to dig into the sand, and within half an hour, they disappeared under the sands and coral.

New York 2 am

"Pull it. What do we have?" On the overhead screen popped the face of Maria.

"We need to build a dossier. Plan Apricot." The plan called for a slow descent into insanity for the target.

Jared turned to Tom, "Oh, vicious. We have not done that for a while. "

"She asks the wrong questions," Tom said.

Jared checked the black web and secret data. "Nothing much, no nudity, no crimes, clean as a whistle."

Tom turned, "Nothing? That's all you can do. Even with all her affairs?"

Jared said, "We used the same process as the Senator last week. Nothing comes up."

Tom sat and threw his cap on the table.

Jared walked over, "Who will get to do the nasty?"

Tom looked out the window, "I might do this one."

Jared said, "Last year with the Governor, we needed some old photos, and they made it detection proof, put false photos out on the net." Jared liked this one, as it was challenging to carry this out and not too fast."

Tom said, "Get to it and don't leave the building until this is done."

4 am—Lord Saxon's back office.

Nobody had ever seen Saxon sleep, ever. "Amir, we are targeting Global News."

Amir nodded, shut down all screen, and lit up the various databases on 20 screens around the room.

Saxon put his hand on Amir's shoulder, "Volatility play. Urgent."

Amir said, "Got it. Building the custom algorithms."

Saxon wrote the media milestones for the next week. "Pump it up today and let it linger two days, then hell breaks loose."

Amir was working the keyboards, "Let us get this stock jumping a bit. Let us ride up a bit."

"Then, we will trigger some hits." Saxon said, "Media companies are tricky. Let's make it all financial and radical alt-media."

Amir said, "Putting the plan in the system, and alt-media will get something out by noon." He looked at Saxon's notes, "We will run it up today and crash it three times in four days."

Later that day, the US-China Global Assets company shifted their holdings on the stock and sent a message secretly to select brokers. A broker on the floor called in the institutions to pull out one percent from their stock holdings of Global News to check the reaction. There was movement on the stock of three percent. Then they pumped it up again and saw the sensitivity that brought the price up to twenty percent.

The next day, the crew canceled ads from TV shows and print and blamed it on the next politician in line for destruction.

Brokers went to work: "Call into the advertising company."

"We need to shift this advertising budget from Global media over to CBD media."

"We will do that immediately. Ok, make the call at 11:55."

Later that day, more bets placed against the stock - 20,000 puts on the stock out over the next six months' price levels. When the stock drops, the firm earns billions.

New York. 9 pm

That day near Broadway and 52nd, Tom sent Timos to trigger contact. He rented an Airbnb under a fake name near Maria's townhouse. Timos had a crew of six that tracked her every action.

Timos, the early thirties, a middleweight boxing contender, rugged and fit – icy eyes, rigid jaw, and clean-cut was a cold, calculating guy - 195 pounds of steel on a six-foot-two frame. He could deadlift his bodyweight three times over. He served two tours in West Africa, taking down some troublemakers, and gained a reputation in the Army as a fierce weapon with no hesitations. He was screened for elite units but could not be controlled and recruited out of the military to this assignment.

Maria stepped out of the townhouse with her boyfriend. The trackers called up to Timos to exit and follow. Timos moved behind and followed them into the LeBron Club on 54th Street.

Timos sauntered up to the bar, leaned against Maria, and stepped on the boyfriend's shoes. He hocked and spit nearby - anything to draw conflict.

Timos pushed her boyfriend, allowed himself to be hit, and nearby the tracker team took photos.

"Oh no, man, what are you doing?" Timos started to trip forward into Maria, provoking a response and negative facial expressions – more photos.

Morning, New York Post.

The next day, photos were on page six of the NY Post - photos of Maria with a scowl. Nothing terribly wrong, but Maria was never in the newspaper like this. It signaled to the industry that Maria was now fair game and other newspapers republished the photos. Paparazzi started tracking Maria with new attention, and not in the way she enjoyed.

The most formidable task was left to Jack, dressed as an everyday unnoticeable dude. The next morning, Jack passed Maria and put a small patch of medicine on her neck. This slowly clouded her thoughts over the next few hours, and Maria started to take risks at work and at night. She went to the club again, and the next day was in the news with more photos of bad behavior.

Maria was to interview the Undersecretary of State for Asia. Ten minutes before the show, fake photos of her in naked positions were put on major alternative sites. She fixed her makeup and saw online a competing major news broadcaster report, "Today we have some exciting news about Maria. Apparently, she has some shocking photos. We will show after the break." On-screen was a photo with a black mark over her privates.

"What? Oh, my God." She bolted to the other room and rewound the program. "Today, we have…."

Maria put her hands to her mouth in shock. "No, no-no." Maria cried and canceled her interview.

She texted her boyfriend. He called. "Maria, what is happening? How did you get photos like that out in the world?"

"I never did this. It is fake!" Maria cried.

"Maria, they have photos on the BLM network. Do you know?" He transmitted the clips to her.

"Oh dear," She stumbled back.

On another show were a beautiful host and her sidekick. They were discussing the photos but teasing the audience. "Sam, I hear you have some exciting news for us this morning."

"Yes, Melanie, I sure do. Maria was caught in a trying position last night. She got into an altercation and struck an elderly woman. Here we have some photos from a few hours ago…." Up popped the image with the lady's face blurred out. This news was fake, built with advanced video and photo software.

Maria cried, "I am ruined!"

One hour later, Maria stepped outside and was hounded by four photographers. They crowded around her as she tried to walk through, and they blocked her, taking photos.

Maria screamed, "Back off!"

They continued taking photos, bumping into her, provoking her. Maria called a taxi. Two of the bullies interfered, paying the taxi driver two hundred dollars to leave without her.

Maria put her head down and walked. They tailed, harassing, and standing in her way. Maria was hounded by paparazzi on mopeds, cars, vans, following her relentlessly. They camped in front of her home day and night.

Maria was anxious and panicked; someone delivered food anytime. Police could not do anything. Her career was failing hour by hour. "What did I do to deserve this? Why all the attention?" Maria fell on her bed and shook.

China

CCTV showed footage from the South China Sea and reported that the USS Trump had destroyed a Chinese Navy ship and killed 33 Chinese sailors.

"Americans are slaughtering our sailors on the island!"

"War Crimes!"

The viewers around China screamed and called for mayhem and justice and revenge and killing white people.

They yelled:

"Social justice!"

"Chinese lives matter!"

Virginia

Joe lived a pleasant hour from civilization.

It was one of the things that drove him to join the military when he was a teen. Now in his late forties with a nice pension and piece of land, he had a perfect house to enjoy with his two children, Tommy, and Mindy. Joe was enjoying a quiet life, off the grid, close to nature, and self-sufficient. He was quite pleased, but Mindy was in the hospital with a disease.

The dogs start barking, and he heard a truck coming up to his door.

"Dad, two guys here look like some of your old friends."

At the door was Tom. They were in the same Special Forces group. Joe was a few years older, less ambitious than Tom.

"Joe, we need you. We are short of people, and the pay is good. We must staff up. There is a giant terrorist cell nearby. If you do not help now, they could come and get you later."

"That is horseshit. You have enough staff for anything." He shut the door.

Tom put his arm to block. "Joe, nobody else knows this area like you. One last time. We will pay you twenty now, and fifty more when it is done."

"Do not need the money, and if I did, you know the government owes me a lot of back pay from that bad discharge."

"We cover all medical bills for Mindy, no matter how much. We will put here at Johns Hopkins and give her all the best. All free, and we will pay off your mortgage. We need you." Tom gave Joe the document showing the terms.

"How do you know about Mindy?"

"Joe, come on," he looked at him with knowing eyes, as if Joe should ever question the government knowing anything or everything about anybody.

Joe was thinking. "Damn medicine was expensive, and there is no way I can afford to put here in Johns Hopkins or any other clinic."

Joe let Tom enter. He went to make more coffee while Tom sat. After a few minutes, "Ok, I am in." Joe wondered if this was going to be his last mission. Now he is back in the system, and who knows where this will take him and family.

The next morning, Joe arrived in Centerville, Virginia. He had the coordinates and target vehicle. He was set up with sophisticated weapons, high powered scope.

A few hours later, he saw the vehicle, "Damn, that is odd."

He lay looking through the rifle scope, checking the targeted terrorist vehicles.

"Damn, that is the President."

"What the hell is that? That is no terrorist. Oh, my God, I am the Patsy." He jumped in the car and raced at full speed. "Damn, damn, these bastards, what is going on!?"

China

Zhang was working on banking reforms to increase the spread of interest across the country.

Fultz, the Deputy NATO Commander, came on the screen and said, "Mr. Zhang, we want to assure you that we will work with you. We have a committee full of our best academics. We will help you to bypass these restrictions that the US Congress set up. Those animals do not deserve any respect, and we will see the day when that silly institution is wiped off the face of the earth. Then we will have sustainable development and prosperity for our offspring."

"Ok, what are the terms?"

Fultz said, "We transfer four key technologies with support to help you deploy. These will bring your operations into space and give balance to the world order. You will be able to defend yourself."

Zhang said, "Of course, we need to defend ourselves. Let's build to coordinate your efforts with the select team that we will set up here."

Lord Saxon entered the conversation, "We will send a special agent to coordinate all actions. You will launch some payloads for us to start to set up the new international space station. After the operation is in place, you will participate in the New World Order as a partner and equal among all."

Zhang smiled, "Perfect plan."

Jones said, "After the operation, you will receive payment for debts owed to you with computer issued Federal Reserve money. This will go directly into your account. You take what you deserve and put the rest into your National State Treasury. You will be able to securitize this against the social security and income taxes we have in place to ensure that tax revenue is raised to collect these funds."

Zhang sat back. "You are great men of world peace."

"We will sign the deal in Switzerland, and debt will be paid in the Bank of International Settlements."

Zhang said, "Thank you. The International Space company needs the high precision GPS controls and other software needed for guidance systems."

Fultz said, "GX company will work with the China Heavy Industries Corporation to set this up."

Zhang said, "We will do a demonstration project on maglev launch soon."

Fultz said, "Your nuclear energy sites are shut down. How will you get the energy for that?"

Zhang said, "We are setting up maglev demonstration projects in every province, but there was lacking some key technology that limits the speeds. And we need information about advanced techniques for launching drones with these rails."

Lord Saxon said, "We have further technology for your maglev demonstration projects in every province."

Zhang said, "This is a small concession for the USA sinking our Navy."

Lord Saxon leaned forward, "This is sensitive technology, but if you agree to support us at the Conference on carbon trading and the New World Order..."

Zhang said, "Yes, we support."

Saxon said, "We will give you the technology this week."

Zhang smiled.

The company

Lord Saxon relied on several companies to carry out his network. GX Tech Corp was a private company of 2400 people. There are just four partners with Justin Kennedy at the top, his brother as the head of finance, his classmate as chief engineer, and one person from Lord Saxon's central organization. Payment for projects was enormous, with the top people getting enough money to buy massive ranches stretching from Texas to Arizona.

Backed by unlimited money printed at will to support any task, these companies were the modern version of Robber Barons. There was no reason to rid this system. It gathered the wealth from society and moved it over to the asset management companies. The critical requirement was silence and loyalty.

GX Tech developed the innovation to take control of cars and trucks autonomously. If anyone stepped out of line, they may come across an unwelcome visitor or found their car doing unusual movements. Space satellites, called SuperPlus, sent commands with technology even the military did not know. These commands could run vehicles off the road or into a barrier under a bridge. SuperPlus satellite systems were now in every car by law and collected hefty monthly fees from car and truck owners.

GX Tech was applying to be listed on the New York stock exchange. Companies like GX recruited heavily fresh out of top schools with very lucrative pay packages. Recruiters looked for smart young graduates with weakness and a need for money at any cost.

At a recent recruiting fair for GX Corp, a gorgeous Chinese woman, about 25 years old, sat across from the candidate. She gave her card and said, "I am here to help with anything you need. My role is to guide you. After a few weeks of orientation, you will be in. There is no question. Not even your wife will know what you do, and she will love the lavish vacations, high status in her community, and pampering every day."

One candidate might ask, "What if I need to leave the system?"

"Why would you ever want to do that? This is what everyone strives for. You do not want to leave the system. This sets you up for life and gives you and your family all the riches you can ever dream about."

That was enough to buy silence.

China

Saxon returned to Beijing to meet President Wang. He brought his best whiskey and cigars.

"You will print money in China based on nothing from thin air." Saxon said, "International financial organizations are used to build a global empire, leading to a dream of real peace. With the paper money system, and now everything going digital, they have unlimited ability to generate money and wealth. Old industries are history. To make a billion in profit, automobile companies had to hire 100 thousand people, set up channels, and make sales and services. Today, I can do that in one minute."

President Wang said, "We know this, but we are not a reserve currency." He pulled out a box of Cuban cigars and offered one to Saxon.

Saxon said, "You will be." Saxon reached behind to show Wang the balance at his bank jump one billion dollars.

"The real generals and emperors have the power to print money." Wang opened the cigar box.

Saxon opened the whiskey and smiled, "30 years bottle. Older than any of my ladies in waiting."

Wang chuckled.

Saxon went on to explain the new system. " That free-market experiment ended over ten years ago during that series of coronavirus pandemics. Nice job." He poured the whiskey.

Wang said, "Of course, we made your governor buy masks from us for one billion dollars."

Saxon laughed, "A great tool that guy was. Too bad, he was assassinated."

Wang said, "Here, with the ministers in place managing significant sectors of the economy, and with unlimited money, technocrats could do the smart work for the people.

Saxon said, "You call them ministers. We call them tsars." They laughed. "With the New World Order, we use the organizations to set up the conditions to make other nations subordinate to the financial organizations."

President Wang stood, "We need guarantees."

Saxon said, "We agree to give you at least 20 percent of the credit structure worldwide. We give you 15 percent ownership in our largest asset management company, Black Granite. You can use that for stock manipulation and list shadows of your companies with BVI and Cayman Island registrations onto the New York stock exchanges. This can allow you to transfer trillions of wealth out of the USA."

President Wang lit his cigar, "One financial weapon we use is loaning to develop infrastructure in South Asia and Africa – Ports, highways, airports, power plants. Any politician who needed some 'encouragement' would get a dose of money. Any project that needed funding, no problem. The politician would have no need for any sort of free-market development for products to be made and then tested in the marketplace.'""

Saxon poured a double shot of whiskey, "Yes, the condition is that individual companies must do the work. So, this is a transfer of the left hand to the right hand. Certain key corporations carry out the work."

Wang leaned forward, "Exactly, the recipient country is then required to pay back all the debt. The debts are designed to become so large that it is impossible to pay back. Then the debtor must give us further concessions in facilities, mineral fields, and such. The debt continues to grow. Debt levels grow astronomically, and it is the cost of servicing the critical debt that puts them in our hands."

Saxon laughed, "You know it! Yes, and get control of labor, install larger income taxes, more fees on homeowners, and healthcare costs. With these projects, all real wealth is diverted to paying off the project itself and servicing the project's debt. A considerable proportion of national wealth is diverted to this effort, and the media helps protect the transfer mechanisms. The only way to pay off the debt under the provisions is to sell off national assets to pay off the debt servicing and principal."

President Wang chuckled, "Your Generals and Admirals still wear uniforms with that silly 'fruit salad' on their chests. Ours too. It is excellent for their labor."

Saxon lit his cigar, "The real modern general no longer wears a military uniform. He uses computers, legal documents, and media propaganda. Appear humble, high class, distinguished, and proper. These new military commanders talk about giving to the poor, foundations, education, and non-profit organizations."

President Wang poured a double scotch. "Thank you for working with me at your level. That President Cortez of yours is pretty weak."

Saxon clicked glasses with Wang. "We will give her more status in the media." He sat back and said, "Forget the American President, whoever it is. The system itself is set up to support these operations. The system is in place to allow these people to go in and transfer wealth legally and systematically to the elite. We have elections to fool the general public. If this does not work, then we have street thugs in a mask, with simple-minded slogans to burn the cities down. Jackals lurk, and they will carry out the violence. If the jackals fail, then war is started."

Wang grabbed the box of cigars and gave to Saxon, "Let's do what we can with our paper and digital money. Now the Hong Kong dollar is tied to the US dollar. These will convert renminbi in secret to HK dollars and then enter the US banking systems."

Saxon lit a cigar. He smiled and said, "Yes, with that money made from thin air, you can buy ten thousand more factories and retail shops in America."

Wang said, "We have tried that, but it is a lot of headaches. Americans have their own ideas and won't follow orders blindly. Damn it, they have guns."

Saxon leaned forward and cut a new cigar, "We will get rid of the guns when the time is right. But this is much bigger, in the hundreds of trillions of dollars. It is a one-time deal and will collapse the system except for something else we have planned."

Wang drank the shot, "What do you have planned?"

Saxon said, "One more shot, let's finish the bottle." And they clicked shot glasses. "You will see it. Trust us on this, and you will see everything we do with you is for the benefit of our elite, the two sides of our political party, You, and the China Communist Party."

John at home

Amy said, "Did you know that the Chinese were in North America a long time before the Europeans came?"

John was eating mashed potatoes and reading his documents, "People crossed the Bering Straits a long time ago."

Amy said, "Not that. In the textbook, the Chinese were in America, and the White men started slavery in 1619. They committed genocide against the Chinese."

John looked up, "nonsense, what are they teaching you at that school?"

Amy said, "It is here in writing with proof from anthropologists."

John said, "Nonsense."

Amy looked at her phone, "These all have PhDs. It is peer-reviewed. It is science. I got a C on the essay because I questioned the facts."

John said, "Facts? Science is always questioning the facts. I have a PhD and know about science."

Amy said, "They have thousands of articles published, and 97 percent of scientists agree."

John looked at her, "So what?"

She showed her phone, "It is science, 97 percent agree. The white man started worldwide slavery in 1619 and committed genocide against Chinese people in North America."

John's phone shook, and he stood.

"John, we have your documents here. Do you have any documents with you?"

"Yes, right here."

"What is the code on the top of page three?"

"X98."

"Where are you?"

"Home."

"Ok, stay there is something to talk with you. Don't go anywhere."

"Ok, no problem," and he laid down on his sofa.

Three minutes later, a hard knock on his door shook John. He opened to see two men and behind them a black van with tinted windows.

They brought John's file. "What did you read?"

John gave them the company file. "Just the first eight pages."

"Ok, that's ok, we just need to know it is for the drill, we have to test everything out, and it's a little like taking your college final, you know?" The guy returned to his black van.

Peggy said, "John, who was that? "

"Oh, just someone from work."

The next day was typical, and John had been a little tense about Amy's low grades and the men at the door. John rewrote his software and adjusted it for the drill, taking the impact of total electricity shutdown and the effects applied to other variables.

His boss came to his door, looking nervous, with another man. "John, could you tell us, I mean, we are here with the movie, we need to know what you read, and ensure that you will not divulge anything."

"Of course, I just read about tonight's show and some things like that." John shifted in his seat.

"Oh, that is a funny part of the movie. You should see where it leads later. It is a real laugher."

John chuckled.

"Ok, John, thank you for your time. I think you are terribly busy with software models. I won't hold you up anymore."

John thought something was a bit disturbing. He worked building the models and running it online with the national lab. He had unlimited funding for overtime and was offered a two-month bonus to his salary to get things working by the end of the week. He stayed in the office most nights testing and tweaking the code with simulations of various scenarios and variables.

The next day, men came back to John with more questions.

"John, Mr. Smith needs to get some information from you regarding the documents you read."

"John, why did you take those documents?"

"It was a mistake; they were on my desk." John knocked his water over on his desk.

"Have a seat."

"Am I being detained? Is there a problem?"

Inspectors, China moves.

The inspectors arrived in Wuhan to check the power plants, the three gorges dam, and high-speed rail. They used Geiger counters to check for nuclear radiation.

The inspectors were treated like kings and loved to visit China. Local officials had an unlimited budget and women to present to the inspectors.

GX

Justin is the CEO of a GX Tech company. At first, a simple company brokering talent between countries helped companies fire high salaried professionals and replace them with low priced outsourced talent. A few times, Justin tried to copy some hot trends into products, anything for an easy buck.

Justin was in Vegas for a trade conference, for superstars under forty. There were thirty of the fast-moving and up and coming CEOs of technology companies. Some tech heavyweights were there, but one of the most interesting speech was given by the CIA's deputy director. There was discussion of private-public partnership, some new tech tying in body frequency with communication, x-rays, splitting frequencies down to a much more acceptable level, and detecting abnormal frequencies. This all to help to track international terrorism and terrorist in the US homeland.

Justin was looking for anything for money and to be the richest in his year group. A 27-year-old programmer gave a presentation of his designs for a competing software package. Justin seethed with rage, envious beyond words. His blood boiled while the programmer received applause. As Justin stood and applauded, his perfect smile and beaming eyes hid vicious hatred, boiling blood, seething rage, and scheming mind.

After midnight, Justin was called to his hotel to meet in two hours. A man drove Justin to near the Nellis Air Force base, where he met a young man from Black Granite venture capital.

"Ok, Justin, this is your lucky day. We are going to turn over some technology to you, which you can claim ownership. You will go to meet your colleague, who we will identify, and give him this file, and sign these documents. This is a sealed envelope. After you receive this, you will be ready to launch a PR announcement in three weeks."

"Yes, of course," Justin said.

"We have already listed you on the Nasdaq market," the man said.

"What? How is that possible?" Justin was shocked.

"Idiot, we are Black Granite."

Justin said, "Oh, I worship you!"

"Look. We will book 12 million in revenue into your books. Your wealth will double overnight. This is guaranteed, and you can claim up to ten percent more ownership of company stock."

Justin tugged his arm, "Whatever you need."

The man said, "We are not playing around. Last week he tried to do a deal but was rejected. You will learn about technology. Your story is that you scoured long and wide and came up with a new heat protecting material that can protect at ten thousand degrees and protect the microchip. this material was proven in explosive tests and other details."

Justin was stunned. "This will change everything."

The man said, "You will be on the way to the top levels. You will get training on talking with the media, and this will make you a billionaire overnight."

Justin stepped back to the car and leaned against it.

"Oh, you will be. You need to fly out in four hours."

"What? I don't have any suits."

"Justin, you be ready in two hours, and we will measure you for suits. You will get those in Beijing."

Justin was stunned but ready for the big world ahead. He was wondering what the material was. It doesn't really matter. He won't even tell his family and friends, and things will come out in due course. That is great - the more, the better. Outer space is there for mass transportation, and we are going to be part of it.

China

China Construction Corporation modified rail lines at 20 locations around China. Each site could change to a slightly curved ramp and long magnetic levitation tube similar to the railguns on the USS Trump – but much more extensive.

A year ago, many of the launchers in the lowlands failed due to wind turbulence. The launchers in Henan exploded. Poor engineering and design made the rods angle off and the crash into farmland twenty miles away, killing half the village there. One rocket exploded in a town and killed over 700 people. This alerted the world to strange activity and raised lots of questions. Hundreds of people died, and the sky lit up with each impact.

It took persistent and intense engineering to fix the situation. The technology transfer from General Fultz and GX Tech was the last needed piece to the puzzle.

Underwater.

Sensors and fake squids continued swimming across the oceans, far and wide, up, and down the deepest canyons of the sea. They sent sonar to find the oceans' submarines.

Off the Coast of Japan

The F55 fighter passed the final inspection and deployed to Japan. It flew successfully with no detection in tests.

China developed stealth drones to track any aircraft. One Friday evening, a stealth F55 fighter trained off the coast of Japan. On the port side, the pilot saw eight drones, "Whoa."

He banked hard, but the drones stayed on his tail. He reported to base, "Alert, I see aircraft on my tail flying at incredible speed and G-forces. I cannot shake the aircraft off."

He checked the radar and saw no aircraft nearby. The drones could fly faster and at much better maneuvers than the F55! The drones were invisible on the radar!

FIVE. DECISIONS

China

President Wang distracted the population from the last war: keep them busy; keep them fed; keep them brainwashed. Best of all, possible outcomes would be a counterattack and massive victory.

Every day, all media in China broadcast reminders of the last war - dead students, humiliation. Xiao Wan was becoming a media star. She moved to Beijing and was on nightly news at 6 pm. Examples of reports would be, "These foreign inspectors come to our country, kill our children." She would weep as before, and this could take a good ten minutes. The anger fed every day, and any dissent was dealt with fiercely. Reports not supporting the approved message brought death to the journalists and their families. Disloyal activists or people who would not yell loud enough approval were collected and sent to reeducation camps. People who fit a specific profile were watched and put into house arrest under guard by area wardens. Some of the suspects were given a bracelet, made of hardened steel, and any attempt to cut was fruitless.

China was getting tired of the inspectors, a holdover from the war, and the media started to demagogue them. The last group was caught on camera in a KTV with young women. The government set aside this KTV to be wiped out, as it was owned by a rival gang that never fit in with the Communist Party. Reports of everything spoke of wild immoral acts.

Ratings were increasing, and people responded, demonizing the attackers.

"These foreigners are cockroaches."

"The foreign devils, the evil people who did this…"

Then on and on and on, this loop would play for hours.

It was especially useful for that half of the population below the average IQ.

New York

Over the next days, the media company was hit with bad earnings reports, improprictics with numbers, and poor accounting practices. Then large advertisers canceled contracts, and shows were suspended. On other network news, late-night talk shows, Wall Street Journal, NY Times, and AP wires reported the 'scandals' at the top of their shows.

The stock price collapsed with calls for the CEO to be fired. He suffered panic attacks and landed in the hospital. He called in the company attorney, "Abe, what is going on? Where is this coming from?"

"Everything leads to a dead end."

"Who is sending out these messages, and how are they?"

Panic selling dropped the stock price by 80 percent. This massive media company brand was crippled. Other firms came with offers to buy the company with pledges to fix the problem and give it a new focus. The financial elite did not care as they owned all media companies, and the loss for one will be won for others – the average was the same. In fact, this scared the hell out of management and kept social issues in order. It was a chance to clean out disloyal people from an organization and move sycophants up the ranks. Chaos and control were the game.

Lord Saxon called the CEO. "Yes, it seems a good idea to get Maria away from NYC with all this rumor and press."

The CEO said, "My God, our stock is tanking."

Saxon said, "Put this Maria reporter on the USS Ford before 7 am tomorrow."

"Where is the USS Ford?"

"Get it done or else."

Within one-hour, Maria was on a chartered airplane to San Diego for the assignment on the USS Ford.

--

Rural China

The maglev rail launchers were designed to send over one ton each into low space orbit. The best launchers were in Tibet, high up in the plateau. With the high-speed rail, pods from Hubei were sent to Tibet, and over 4000 pods were lined up at three launchers. These pods were twice as big with long telephone pole size rods with markings as parts of the International Space Station.

The energy needed for each launch was enormous—about one gigawatt-hour dedicated to each launch. The equipment to gather this and deliver the power was spread all around the launch. It was still underground in a series of 40-foot containers full of mechanical flywheels and huge energy storage containers, buried over the previous six months.

For days, every farm and power plant in rural China ran at a full generator to produce energy. This energy carried over to the local grid through peer to peer networks across the parallel electric lines and electric train networks. The energy pumped water into all lakes above dams so that they could run full load later. Massive storage batteries tied in with certain parts of the train lines were full and ready to feed vast energy.

The call went out nationwide for heavy-duty trucks to report to their local security bureau.

Xiao Chen woke to a message: Move to the train station at 6 am

In his truck chassis, they were the new frame system made from composite ceramics carbon and tungsten. These were strange components, an experiment in modular manufacturing and materials - one of the lightest and most rigid materials on the planet now. Pretty expensive and not well received, but there they were in the trucks. Now the call was put out to collect this item – over a million of them. They were gathered up and told to ship them to twenty sites around the country.

"My God, so early." He dressed and drove his 18-wheel truck to the station, and security directed him to a warehouse where he lined up. He stepped down, and a guard gave him a voucher for ten thousand renminbi and coupons for breakfast.

Soldiers took his truck to an area where four rods were removed from the suspension and replaced with regular steel beams.

Once at the site, they were put through an inspection, and housing put on the back, superior welding put on them in factories nearby. The rods moved to a second station. A thin layer of tungsten was fit onto the spear; on the front fixed a super hard tip; on the back was welded a computer control set of fins, about five pounds—the precise fins made from some of this new material from the GX Tech company.

Lined up in warehouses near each site and covered overhead to hide from satellite detection were thousands of these pods. China had produced more than 30,000 pods and could make 5,000 per month. The country was working at full employment, and the Army was exceptionally busy.

The spears moved to the next station and placed 19 others into a larger vessel shaped like a rocket. Within each vessel was a series of rods reinforced with tungsten tips. The rods converted to long cylinders with a sharp nose and thin retractable wings. Each weighed from 20 to 2000 pounds.

Chen waited at a tea house, watching movies. After four hours, he received the truck and a voucher to accept a new 400 square foot apartment as payment – one hundred feet per rod. Chen was quite pleased.

Switzerland

A video conference call was arranged with Zhang, Jones, Saxon, and the Senator.

"Your main task here is to push onto States a vast portfolio of loans," Zhang said.

Jones said, "Yes, we know."

Saxon broke in on the video, "Then these loans will be used to hire companies from our network. We cannot have so much power under control with States like Texas, Montana, and Nevada. The loans will be impossible to pay off after going through a series of cost overruns and other arrangements. Then we can start to negotiate terms with the States as soon as they are forever in our debt."

"Senator, you use your statistical modeling and arts of persuasion to show that these projects will bring about enormous growth in GNP."

"If things do not go well, you turn it over to the central team. They have the people in place that can help you to persuade." Saxon closed his video.

Justin Corp

Everyone in Justin Corporation had increased perks and salary: extravagant expense budgets, unlimited, and no reason to stray from the path. Everyone was there to build up the empire, do their part, and serve the corporate interest.

Justin was in Beijing at a banquet celebrating the technology transfer. The banquet table held twenty people, fifteen Chinese and four Americans. Justin sat next to President Wang. Wang asked Justin, "I heard there are people in your cities who will stage riots and bring down leaders that they do not like. If they need, they will burn an entire apartment building to kill a Mayor that does not agree with their beliefs."

Justin nodded his head, "It is a distraction. Our goal is to push all wealth into the hands of a few."

Wang replied, "Yes, just a few, and you included. The general population will learn to make do with the new Order. We will bring about a new Order for the World."

Justin said, "I tell my company 'this is about the survival of the fittest.' We are the fittest."

Wang said, "The elite will rule the world because we are superior to the masses.

Justin nodded, "Some people want to be slaves, and some want to rule. We will rule."

Wang said, "You have learned. The select few need to gather resources and control. This is our God-given right, Justin. War and famine are there to clean out the middle class and put them in line to be our servants."

Justin smiled, "We offer you the technology for the guidance and heat-resistant material."

Wang stood and raised his glass, "Cheers. My billionaire friends."

South China Sea

The snake devices from the sunken ship burrowed underground. They stretched to under the ground across the center of the island. The machines started to shake and created vibrations, which caused the soil and material to liquify.

The islands became worthless. American sailors measured these and understood there were metal cylinders with low vibrations liquifying and making the islands melt back into the sea.

Sand at water's edge school and created quicksand. The concrete and asphalt of the airstrip started to crack.

Similar devices were activated in Guam and Subic Bay, and Bremerton Washington. There was no way to get to these devices as they liquified the earth and sank the structures above.

USS FORD

Maria arrived by helicopter on the USS Ford, an aircraft carrier, the greatest warship ever built, 20 miles out to sea beyond San Diego.

"Madam, come to the galley, and we will get you coffee."

The wind picked up and pushed Maria. They moved below deck to a quiet area.

Maria was angry and decided to mock the interview, caught on civilization's outskirts on a 100-thousand-ton monster ship. Maria asked, "How wonderful are you to command this aircraft carrier?"

The USS Ford is the latest and most incredible ship ever built. 13 billion dollars of US taxpayer money.

Maria ended her interview in a minute, wrote her article, and went to sleep depressed.

White House, morning briefing

Johnson read the technology and the troop
movements and put this information together.

"Madam President, we are getting a lot of
strange reports from various sectors."

"Well, this one is the space launch on
schedule," Cortez said.

"But the launch is coming from twenty
different locations."

"Sure, that is the launch. Well, you know
Chinese are very industrious." Cortez poured
her coffee.

"We need to escalate this now."

Underwater probes

The squids swam quite efficiently, indetectable
from familiar creatures, and were in sight of the
submarines. They glided serenely to the
submarine and then within ten feet, spread out
six long legs, and grabbed hold of the sub.

The crew knew there was an object attached to
the outside, but at that point, it was too late. If
they understood the weapon/squid's nature,

their only chance was to surface and escape. There was no way to unhook the squid. The glue there was as if soldered to the vessel itself.

"Sir, we have an object attached."

"Sir, we are getting reports from all submarines that there are objects attached to their vessels. Some say abnormal activities, all subs are affected."

"Call the Admiral, alert all commands."

China

Zhou and Wang were walking at Zhong Nanhai.

Wang said, "Bring America to its knees. We will take out its satellites and own all its roads and land."

Zhou said, "This small CubeSat solved our problems.

Wang said, "Launch. The next battlefield and be their sunset. Their nation goes to sleep, and their generals wear their fruit salad on their chests. Old men did not grow up with the new tech. They do not understand what their young junior officers understand."

Zhou said, "Classic. The Generals build old equipment, make last century decisions, and persecute those with new ideas."

Wang said, "and then it is over. The battle for space dominance is about to begin."

"We will never be defeated."

TV News

The news anchor turned in his chair, "This just in. A massive solar flare was just released from the sun."

Estimates have it hitting the earth in four hours.

Take precautions and turn off your electronics between the hours of..."

John remembered this was the exact words from the script. He thought, "Well, should go home and round up the kids." He stopped by the boss' office to check out and saw the boss was gone.

The TV announcer turned to an expert, "This is an important story, and this could have significant repercussions for our way of life. "

Simmons from NASA is on the line. Simmons, what can you tell us about these flares?" Well, Bill, the sun is emitting numerous very high-powered bursts that are hitting the solar system. So far, we are only on alert that one can beat the earth but looks like it will pass by us 20 thousand miles away.

What do you hear about the impact?

Well, Sam, even at 20,000 miles, it will have a massive impact on the earth. It will disrupt satellites and could harm some electronics. There will be a briefing in 30 minutes about preparedness.

"Thank you."

Take precaution and turn off your electronics between the hours of .... 6 pm and keep off for 24 hours.

We will notify you by air horn if there is a reason to panic. Take the following precautions ….

John, go-ahead home and spend the next few days with your family. "

John drove home to take it easy, have a nice dinner, and use the microwave for the last time in a day or so. He had candles ready and would enjoy some card games with Amy and Peggy.

John walked to the TV and saw the same solar flare that he remembered from the videos in the office. John felt a sense of superiority, knowing that, unknown to the country, all the images were made in the lab. All media outlets carried the same pictures his company had organized from the design studios in Hollywood and other places.

"This drill will shut down the electric grid for a few hours, and some areas for a few days. We need to monitor how the reactions are and how your model works. To test it, we need to have you not here."

John thought that was odd. "How are they going to fix the software if there is a glitch? Many things could go wrong with the code."

Amy called, "Dad, please come home."

On the way home, John turned on the radio and heard the announcements get gloomier.

On his phone, he told Amy, "Let me pull into the fruit stand and pick some stuff up." There the place is packed like made, and some panic sets in there. John is a bit amused as the script calls for a near miss and nothing to worry about.

"It will all be over tomorrow. In any case, there is no flare. What am I thinking?"

He took in the stressed look on people's faces and saw the value in the drill. "Right old department of homeland security. They really know how to put things together."

At the counter, he heard the radio talk show host say, "this flare is a false flag event be careful of your government staging some false event to bring down the economy."

What a freak - paranoid nuts everywhere. John looked and saw about 20 people listening intently to it, profoundly believing the rants. "Do you believe that?"

They look at him. "Who the hell are you? Yes, it's something to be wary of, do not know about the plans to take down the economy? "

"What are you talking about?"

"Wow, I cannot believe people think this way. "

"Ok, man, whatever." John was genuinely amused and just packed his groceries and went back to his car. He drove home, and then they take it easy- nice dinner, last time to use the microwave for a day or so and sit down and enjoy a night at home.

The solar flare shown on TV was enormous. John knew and was feeling a bit powerful that it was all unknown to the audience. All the images were made in the lab. All media outlets carried the same pictures issued by the international space administration.

John arrived home, and Amy and Peggy were watching the television.

"He watched the TV, saw the various commentators, and stayed up and saw the late-night talk show comedians with the same jokes and banter in the script. He thought, "Ha-ha, the script is really going as planned. It is incredible to see how contrived all this is, how much the media will report straight off a script and keep a straight face."

"Honey, we must shut off the TV at four."

Peggy was at the stove, "John, it is not going to happen."

"They will be monitoring our meter for electric usage. We need to have absolutely nothing working tonight, no ac, no refrigerator. We must shut off the circuit breakers."

"You said it is a drill."

"Peggy, you are not supposed to know that. Who told you that? "

"John, you did a few days ago. You don't remember."

John was shaken by his own loose lips." In any case, they will be monitoring us. What do you think happens if I am using any electricity, and I am part of the management? "

"John, do not worry so much."

"Peggy, this is serious."

He went over to flip the switch, "Peggy, make sure you never mention this to anyone. I will lose my job".

"Of course, John, you can trust me. "

The news programs covered this full time. Everyone is a little nervous, but they are watching the TV. The announcer said, "It looks like the flare will hit the north part of the Earth and affect much of the northern hemisphere. There are a series of flares."

The expert added, "This is from the international space agency. There are six large flares and a series of smaller ones. They are sure to knock out any satellites in their path. "

John remembered the entire script, and it was happening as written in advance. He knew this was a drill, but he is still a little tense. How will people react to the event? Will there be chaos? Well, anyway, I am ready, and nothing will happen.

Submarine

Deep in the trench, the nuclear submarine USS Carter floated quietly. A nine-month tour on this massive machine was leisurely on the crew as they had the latest technology. It was the third part of the nuclear triad and preserved the balance among the nuclear states.

They sat and waited as probes moved as squids closer to the submarines.

These probes were sent with a network of data that was collected by thousands of probes and sensors. Now the submarine was a target, and these two squids found their new home.

The petty officer checked the waveforms of sound helped with artificial software that sifted through billions of data points.

The first squid landed on the sub, checked the temperature and materials, and went into action. The device spread its flaps, and thousands of Velcro-like needles pushed into the submarines shell. The squid device became one with the surface.

"Sir, we have a problem."

China

On the day of the big launch, much more energy fed the containers. Thousands of cars and generators on farms were burning biofuels and converting their engine power into magnetic power. Many vehicles took off the rear wheels and put on rotating disks that acted as power plants. They fed into the local grid, excessed the containers, and converted the energy into a higher voltage. This traveled to substations that gathered the power for transfer over to a container full of flywheels. As each launch happened, the flywheels quickly released their load onto the maglev.

The rods were fit onto the launch pad. With a burst of energy, it launched like a railgun over 1200 miles per hour with a POP sonic boom. Each vessel curved upward until it reached 20 miles above the earth. At that point, a small rocket boosted it to orbit where it waited - quietly.

Then they charged the launcher. This happened all night long, each launcher shooting about one thousand of these loads into orbit - about 20,000 in total. They were launched in quick succession, about one every thirty seconds. There were 22 launch systems throughout the country, and each was assigned a type of material to launch into space.

The rail catapult was 8000 meters long and shot the crafts 1200 miles an hour. Each rod had a little booster rocket and some chips. Those chips housed a GPS, some sensors, and then each rod had fins. These are the housings put on back in each location. Three of the four were preprogrammed with a specific target to hit. The fourth kind was a new version that could roam in orbit and hit targets on the fly.

In a day, tens of thousands of these rods found an orbit to float 'peacefully.'

Colorado

"Hey, what is that?" asked a sergeant in the US Space Command. "There is a very unusual activity in China."

"Oh, that is the Chinese New Year. Some impressive new fireworks.

"This is different, hundreds of large items going into sub orbit and getting to a fixed location."

"Let me see."

"Send this up for further review."

"Turn on all the satellites, call in the analysts."

"Raise an alert now."

Another officer tracked cube satellites designed to move up close to another satellite and attack. He saw on the computer screens one satellite turn off.

He sipped his coffee and adjusted the monitor. Then more satellites turned off in rapid succession.

"Quick," he yells to the control room. He pushes the alert. The computer sends an alert tracking fifty thousand commercial and military objects orbiting the earth and the visual of satellites and objects as small as an inch across. Artificial Intelligence monitors the items and sends alerts for any problems.

A Chinese satellite has been moving through Space and getting close to various of its own military satellites listening to what communications are flowing. This capability was improved so that the satellite releases a small ball which floats to the military satellite. This ball has the satellite's unique identifier, and with a command, it turns on magnets. Individual magnets allow it to accelerate, and then it hits the satellite and explodes, wiping out the satellite.

The time came for the Chinese carrier satellites in orbit to release thousands of balls and with the unique identifiers for American, Russian, British, Japanese, and other countries satellites. These balls kept an orbit around enemy satellites to gather information.

But they had the other ability to approach and, with explosives, destroy the enemy satellites with that technology paid by General Zheng enough to allow the contractor to pay his student debt.

There is no way to know if they are routine communications or a space kill vehicle.

These massive Space kill vehicles with thousands of pods could wipe out communications at will.

Then they made a far more secret. It could grab hold of a satellite and move it out of the way to clean up the area.

Space debris moves so fast that it can randomly kill spacecraft, so this is a peaceful technology.

Madam President, the starts of major wars are silent, but they have their own echo.

The First World War was boots marching; the Second World War was aircraft dive bombing or the atomic bomb; the Third World War could be an unheard sound in Space or software that kills our electric grid, or hackers.

Perhaps a satellite that looks and acts like a communications satellite but is a massive military weapon. Or a space station that is designed to drop to earth and hit a city.

"My God! The next war could be happening right now, and we don't hear it. It could be harmful software in the system or Chinese companies listed on the US stock exchange pilfering the nation's wealth. Later, it could be the railguns you used that started the war, and you don't know it.

It could be domestic terrorists destroying communities and using lasers to blind our officers.

The GPS constellation is the most important network of satellites in Space today. If we lost this, it would go far beyond mapping.

The timing ability affects all our ATMs and keeps our power plants running and checks for errors. We have lost our old systems to monitor, and without GPS, we do not have backup systems. It would undoubtedly affect our military on the ground. Our missiles and bombs would lose their accuracy.

What would it look like without Space if that capability were gone and go back fifty years? An adversary that knocks us out of Space and takes over cannot be defeated. It is a kill shot.

Just the lost early warning of a nuclear attack puts us at the mercy of not knowing.

Now, these missiles can fly in half an hour and strike anywhere in the USA.

Drones

On the launch pads, drone carriers launched.

These space drones can launch and return from space. It takes off in the desert with maglev that sends it up a curved track that kicks it thousands of feet and 1000 MPH, where small booster rockets put it into orbit. This can deliver the massive amounts of goods that we need to the moon or just to space stations.

In the Whitehouse

"War in Space would put so many small items in orbit that could take out the typical spacecraft." General Skykes said.

The President said, "We have a treaty."

"Yes, we have a treaty. But if the other side thinks they can get away with taking a chance, they will do so. The treaty is useless. They could send bio war into the country, and if no real response, they will make space war".

"They would not do that. We have a peaceful coexistence." President Cortez walked around the room.

"But this time with no rules and no limits to what can be done. A so-called social scientist will look at humans as numbers and data. A wicked social scientist will rationalize that the ends justify the means. A population on early of one billion is the right amount."

"There is no deterrence in their mind if they are killing their own people and consuming their own people's resources. They have no limit, no deterrence, Madam President!"

"You are mad," Cortez went behind the desk.

Under the ocean.

The entire USA, UK, French, Russian, and Australian submarine fleets were all discovered by the probes and now had the squid-like devices fused on their hulls.

In defense agencies worldwide, news started to come forth out of secrecy. It took time for the navies to talk with each other about this unusual situation. One sub surfaced, and the Navy found that the remote-controlled squid-like weapons that swim up to the submarine and attached to the hull.

The frequency was sent to a control center in Shandong. As the specialists pulled the device from the submarine, the device bowed up and a sharp phosphorous chemical burned through the hull. The men near the device were burned. A medic and explosive ordnance team rushed forward. In the squid was a nuclear rod heated with the phosphorus and now drilling through the hull. The specialists could not get close to the intense heat. The squid device evaporated. The nuclear fuel penetrated and ignited the submarine's insides with a 10,000-degree heat source that started a massive fire. Within one minute, the entire submarine was in flames.

Backyard.

Dad, come outside and check the solar flare."

"Oh, that is fake….

"John was about to tell her that it was a simulation only, and nothing would happen.

"Don't be silly. Get away from your work."

John looked at his watch, and he remembered that the flares would hit at 4:25 pm. He looked at a squirrel and flicked the TV set on the outside porch to catch the news script. He could see the reporters were reading the exact script as he remembered.

John watches as the reporters show various simulations of the flare precisely as he saw it in his office.

Amy said, "Wow, this is amazing how they can set up the media and show such vivid images."

John recognized the exact shape of the third flare how it popped out of the sun, and he remembered the perspective of the burst as it was viewed from telescopes near the moon. "Wow, what a spectacular show."

"Yes, it is Daddy, and I hope it doesn't hit."

"Don't worry, dear."

He walked to turn off the TV program.

"Daddy, can't we keep watching, or do we have to turn things off?" Amy pleaded.

"Ok, let's turn it off and go out back for a picnic.

"Yes, the girls ran outside and were playing with the water hose." And Amy …

"Whoa, what was that?"

Up in the sky, a bright flash.

Amy said, "Dad, the flares hit!"

John was shocked, "How did they do that?!"

Six nuclear weapons exploded above the Earth.

SIX. RESOLVED

USS FORD

"Maria, you can't help yourself."

"What is it now?"

"Your squitter account you call the USS Ford a 100-thousand-ton floating penis."

"Well, that is a symbol of male prowess. I think the nation will like that."

"Maria, you mock, and the two nuclear power plants are testicles."

"Yes, I thought you would like that. It is for you, my boss."

"Maria, you are destroying us here. And the aircraft and missiles are ejaculate!!"

"That one is for Lord Saxon." Maria smiled.

"Maria, you are fired!!"

Maria stood and turned off the phone, and to the cameraman said, "Well, out with a bang. My work is finished. When can I leave?"

As Maria sat on the helicopter about to lift off, pleased to leave this assignment and job but thinking, "Who will hire me now? What else can go wrong?"

EMP

Six nuclear warheads were lost three weeks ago. They were hidden as part of the International Space Station, and now 35 megaton bombs orbited the earth - ready to go. They were launched from Belgium and controlled from within the NATO structure.

Within NATO was a debate about the future of the alliance. The trend toward expansion included the Middle East, South Asia, and China to clear out all terrorists' world and set up the New World Order. NATO would become a worldwide police force. Ten regions with a top-down ruling committee of 12 wise men would make all decisions. The time had come to save the world from humanity and clear out disease, waste, and corruption - those corrupt being the unenlightened who did not enrich the 'elite.'

Earlier in the week, many parts of NATO command rose the alarm that six nuclear weapons had been moved, and it was a frantic search worldwide. The head of NATO, General

Amos, called for accounting and was working non-stop. Then one day, he suffered a stroke and was now in a coma.

The six nukes deployed.

When the virtual solar flares were designed to hit the earth as part of the drill, these nukes exploded in orbit. The first nuke went off above North Carolina at 4:25 pm. The second one at 4:28 above Nebraska. These caused an enormous electromagnetic pulse that knocked out nearly the entire US electrical grid. The utilities were told to keep their grid alive as this would be a drill – but were they surprised. Every above-ground transmission line and substation were either fried or knocked offline. Most power plants became toast - the inner workings fried. Enough of the grid, substations, transformers, and equipment were, dead, and destroyed. Lights across America went out. Communications and media were nearly all dark.

"Ph, wow, quite a drill." Amy took videos of the flashes and weather. She uploaded, but the network was down.

"Give it some time. The flares are finished soon." John said.

To the people on the ground, this fits in well with the 'drill.' Most of them were ready for this and had turned off their electricity.

"It's part of the 'drill,'" John stared frozen. "Either that is a really realistic drill. It makes no sense. Those flares really hit us hard. That was something."

Most of his neighbors were amazed or nervous at the skylights – nothing ever was seen. Many people had not protected their electronics in their homes and car, and now they had a bunch of equipment that could not work.

Financial markets depend on the exact timing provided by GPS, and they are exposed to interruptions. Now trades sneak in and buy a d sell at artificial numbers, and all stocks are transferred to new accounts. This is much more than a simple cyber-attack.

Traffic lights and signals that are controlled by computers start to break.

Commercial air traffic is stalled. The data is off track; pilots lose navigation, weather data fails, and water breaks down. Sewer systems stop, and valves lock. The massively efficient infrastructure optimized for that last bit of profit margin now gives way to failure. The ghost of reality stomps on the systems that keep these in place.

The armed forces receive the same problems on their bases, and their phones are down.

Air Force pilots and drones lose contact, and GPS guided everything is not working.

In the ocean, the warships lose contact. Critical infrastructure and disable and destroy satellites

crucial missions ranging from commanding nuclear warfare to cyber warfare to war in space anytime human beings have come

They should hope that was the only trick. Next was a rain of hell.

Colorado

The transmission from orbit was alive. The massive blasts disrupted the earth, but, still, all the communications got through to the control center's hardened military equipment.

"Sir, these supply pods are opening, and we don't know what material is there."

"We are hit with EMP waves. This is not a drill."

"The pod is expanding, it looks like it is stretching out, and there are a series of poles on them that are pointing down.

"Take a closer look," the sergeant pointed the optics and focused on the supply pod.

"This is strange, looks like a long rod, with a tip, and on the back, there is some mechanism."

"Run a spectrum scan,"

"We cannot detect any radiation or chemicals. We cannot detect any lasers, chemicals, or nukes. They can't be lasers. It is all inert, just a tiny bit of electricity coming off them."

"What is the material.

"Sir, the frequency shows, some sort of tungsten alloy, with carbon, and there is a chemical coating, something I can't recognize,"

"Send it up for analysis."

"Sir, these are all now vertical, the pod has spread out, and about 100 vertical items there."

"The computer shows heat resistant, chemical compound, from WO84736662 patent." The computer compared the results across many databases.

"Damn, heat resistant, these things only need that if they are coming through the atmosphere."

"Shit- alert, alert!!!!" They sounded the alert. "Send to all levels – open non-secure!!"

"What is this, what is it for?" Everyone was yelling, and some moving. Panic started to set in…

The spears tilted down. Detached, and started their descent. The camera caught the rods detach and fall to the earth. "They are BOMBS!"

Calls go up the chain, and to the President, all bases are alerted. DefCon Five. "All aircraft launch, we are under attack!"

The supply pods opened over the next hour, releasing 20,000 pods over the Northern Hemisphere to the USA, Canada, UK, Russia, Japan, and India.

Over Wyoming, three pods released their spears in succession. These targeted the Cheyenne mountain headquarters in a series. The first one hit and shook the insides, followed by twenty more on target. The next one hit ten seconds later near the same spot, then three more, and now the hole was getting deeper and broader. Massive alerts go off. More hit.

Spears came and punched through the granite. The massive steel gate buckled, and heat started to warp it.

Then a batch of three more. Now the mountain is getting hammered, smashing, and smashing. More hit, another three minutes, and twenty more spears hit. Inside it is getting unbearable. People have concussions, convulsions… eardrums are busted. One punches through, and the energy starts to vaporize everything inside.

After twenty minutes, the final spears hit, and every single living being, every insect within 500 meters is gone. Fried. No nuclear radiation, just granite dust.

Whitehouse.

The Chief of Staff ran into the oval office. "We lost communications with most bases, and Cheyenne Mountain is getting hit with ordnance.

President Cortez said, "The flares affected them. It is a drill."

"Shit, those were not flares; those are nukes. Activate." The Secret Service grabbed Cortez and rushed her to the elevator and base underground.

Various locations under the ocean.

With the unusual devices attached to the submarines, all submarines rose to the surface, and the crew started to abandon.

The activation signal spread worldwide for the squids to deploy their weapons. The intense nuclear heat cut through the hulls and heated the inside to boiling, followed by water rushing into the breach. Every nuke sub was destroyed. In less than five minutes, all submarines of all English-speaking countries, Russian and Japan, were destroyed.

China

A series of drone carriers were launched from the maglevs up to 20,000 feet in a swarm. From there, solar and batteries kept them afloat.

USA

On CNN, reports showed comets hitting Scott Air Force Base near Saint Louis. The signal went to bluescreen.

On the ground, "Look, Mom, comets are coming. Look at the fireworks!"

Ten seconds later, the sound waves reached,

BAM!

"Whoa, what is that?"

The rods screamed downward, accelerating to hyperspeed with small rockets giving a boost. By the time they hit the ground, the spears were going Mach 20. The tungsten and carbon steel were a fiery metal, hitting the earth at 20,000 miles an hour. The force was power of thousands of tons of TNT, like a small nuke. The spears penetrated the ground and shattered anything underground up to 500 feet. It was a massive display of energy.

BAM BAM BAM BAM.

"My God, quick inside!!" the mother pulled her hard.

At the nearby military base controlling intercontinental ballistic missiles. "Sir, malfunction on the radar. It's going on the fritz. Something wrong." The radar system jumped wildly.

Then swoosh, splash, meteorites came.

"What is that?"

Then the room shook hard, with heat pulsing through, wicked ear-busting metal destruction. A spear hit direct and vaporized everyone in the building.

More trouble

Two nukes that went off over the USA knocked out 70 percent of the power grid, and the grid that did work only covered a few small rural areas.

Canada was affected, especially in the East. All long-distance transmission lines were out. All substations, transformers, and most other equipment were gone.

In addition to the two nukes that went off over North America, four more nukes exploded. The third nuke went off over Osaka and covered most of Japan, the fourth over Birmingham, the fifth over New Delhi, and the final south near Moscow.

These attacks were a complete surprise. China targeted eight thousand spears for those countries and destroyed 90 percent of the military capabilities. Within one day, the Chinese New Year of all time, America, Russia, and the UK were brought down. Japan was subdued.

"You must get to safety in the bunker." The Secret Service grabbed the President and dragged her to the train.

Once on the train, the advisor grabbed her coat, "Madam. President, this is real. We are under attack."

You wake up now! The President was in a catatonic state almost.

President regained a clear mind. They hear faint booms above.

The President and security were running underground when the nukes went off. They jumped on the high-speed rail, whisked away toward the offsite command bunker.

President Cortez was sweating, agitated, and hyperaware of everything around her. She is looking at his advisors and secret service agents for safety. "Who did it, where did it come from?"

The advisor said, "Two nukes, one over us and one over Denver."

Cortez said, "Fucking drill!! Who is behind this? Could it be the Chinese, pentagon coup, My God, how can this happen?" She was clearly agitated.

One advisor was panicked and shaking, "This must be a drill. This must be a drill. This can't be real."

"Damn it, shit! What is wrong with that guy? Is he out of his mind? We are under attack! This is not a drill. This is real."

She gets to the command center. In five more minutes, things will really get direr. Five more minutes and the planes gone, the silos gone, the strategic assets wiped out.

Calls came from Cheyenne, then cut out. The map showed an overlay of strategic capabilities, with marks indicating they were damaged or wiped out. Army bases like Fort Hood were untouched, as none of Fort Hood tanks and artillery had any value in this type of war.

"Madam President, we must move. This city is in danger of nuke. They grabbed again and called the helicopter.

USS FORD

Maria followed and return to the deck. "Yes, Maria, you are a fine writer. We have a helicopter leaving now." She hopped on board and the helicopter lifted.

Miles above, the vessel opened and dropped its payload of twenty spears. Each spread out with a target below off the coast of San Diego. One spear was set to meet the 20 billion dollars USS FORD with all its missiles and F55 aircraft sitting pleasantly that day.

At that time, the alarms sounded, and people deployed to their stations.

Onshore in San Diego, people looked out across the ocean and saw what appeared to be comets raining from the sky.

One spear screamed past the ship and splashed water hundreds of feet in the air on the USS Ford, shaking the entire ship.

Maria watched the aircraft carrier as they rose - the excellent aircraft carrier in a storm of spears. She screamed, "Oh God, what is that?"

The spear kicked in with a thrust which pushed it to ten miles per second by the time it hit the ship. Now this spear was only one hundred pounds, but there was nothing that the mighty 20-billion-dollar Navy ship could do with that speed and trajectory.

The spear struck the deck with such speed and mass to kill nearly everyone on the ship.

Then flash, BAM, almost like a nuclear weapon. A spear hit the deck one-third of the way in and created a massive explosion. The ship was pushed down in the water, and 100 thousand tons of ship leapt up out of the water, and buckled. Then it rolled to its side and sat crippled and on fire.

Maria watched from the helicopter above. The flash and boom shook the helicopter and caused them to almost crash.

She saw the carrier on fire, hundreds of sailors dead, all aircraft blew off the deck. She could not hear anything and grabbed her ears and saw she was bleeding.

The helicopter circled to collect more information. The spears stopped falling, and the carrier was on fire and ruined.

The hull buckled and broke. Aircraft were strewn across the water. A few escort ships approached to collect survivors.

The pilot gained command, and they flew to San Diego as Maria watched the spears drop and wipe out all ships in view. As they approached the naval base, she saw the entire Naval Base on fire, and all vessels sunk.

The ship became a towering hulk crippled in the ocean, on fire, and people scrambling. In the sea were bodies.

Then snap, the horrible sound of the hull breaking part. Ripping metal and water rushing in. Sailors jumped, some into the flaming water, they can see a massive fire start to develop. As the reactor is breached. The core heats up, and the fire was reaching hundreds of feet.

The helicopter banked and fled. Maria was thrown against the wall and passes out.

Then the ship's nuclear reactor exploded shooting fire 1000 feet into the sky, the fire expanded outward, and the USS Ford sank.

White House.

"Our Navy is gone. All our F55s are destroyed by drones." The situation became clear.

President Cortez was horrified. "How could this happen? So fast! General, do something. Get some retaliation. What is going on? This damn communication channels."

He grabbed the nuclear football and ready to launch, but to where? What did we have left? How did we not see this coming?"

She answered the phone: "We overrode the codes. Do not do anything, and you will be fine."

Senator Mitch moved in to see the President. The news came in, "lost contact with the submarines, Madam, it looks like they have been attacked."

President Cortez sat and said nothing.

"We get readings of explosions and distress on the submarines. We cannot contact most of them, and three that we have contact with say their hulls have been breached. They are all sinking!"

"Madam President, alert!"

"Full alert!"

"Navy to launch all missiles," Cortez said.

"The subs and ships and planes are all gone. We have no missiles."

"Madam President, President Wang is on the phone."

President Cortez froze. She looked at the Chief of Staff and took the phone.

President Wang said. "We have many more bombs to drop and can hit you in one minute."

Cortez said nothing and sobbed.

Wang said, "Can you control your military?"

Cortez said, "Yes."

Wang said, "We will collect reparations from your middle-class population. Can you control your population?"

Cortez said nothing.

Wang continued, "We can hit you in one minute. All we want to know is, can you ensure that the general population is kept under control and not aware of their new masters?"

Cortez said, "Yes."